I am a grown-up.

Her wish had come true!

Then Jenna opened her eyes. *This is really my office!* she thought, gazing around in awe. There was a framed diploma on the wall. "I got a Bachelor of Arts in communications," she whispered, touching the glass with her fingertip. "Wow." And what a view! The people down on the street looked like ants from up here. One of the walls had shelves, and there were tons of framed photographs. There was Jenna—the grown-up Jenna—dancing with Lucy; then standing next to a man with brown hair; then standing next to a man with blond hair; and in a third picture, standing with the man from the shower! *Is he my boyfriend?* Thank heavens he had clothes on.

Then Jenna gasped. There was a picture of her with Madonna! Scrawled across the photograph in black ink were the words *Jenna girl, margaritas anytime! Love ya, Madonna.*

"I'm friends with Madonna?" Jenna said, stunned. *We drink margaritas together?*

Things were even more awesome than she had ever imagined.

13.
going
on 30

13. going on 30

A Novel by Christa Roberts

Based on the Motion Picture Screenplay by
Cathy Yuspa & Josh Goldsmith and Niels Mueller
Story by Cathy Yuspa & Josh Goldsmith

bantam books
new york—toronto—london—sydney—auckland

AGES 12 AND UP

13 Going on 30
A Bantam Book/April 2004

ISBN: 0-553-49462-7

Visit us on the Web! www.randomhouse.com/teens
Educators and librarians, for a variety of teaching tools,
visit us at www.randomhouse.com/teachers

Published simultaneously in the United States and Canada

Bantam Books is an imprint of Random House
Children's Books, a division of Random House, Inc.
BANTAM BOOKS and the rooster colophon are
registered trademarks of Random House, Inc.

PRINTED IN THE UNITED STATES OF AMERICA

10 9 8 7 6 5 4 3 2 1

for O and W . . . don't grow up too fast.

● ● ● foreword

You may have seen TV specials or heard stories from your parents about the eighties. It was a time of big hair, acid-wash jeans, and actual music videos on MTV. There was no Internet, no e-mail, and no cell phones. No ATMs. No DVDs. No SUVs.

No cordless phones.

And no reality TV.

That's when this story begins, in 1987.

The year Jenna Rink turned thirteen.

But that's not quite where it ends. . . .

13.
going
on 30

● ● ● one

Jenna Rink picked up her packet of school pictures and smiled politely at the PTA mom behind the table that had been set up in the school hallway. "Thanks." Holding her breath, she pulled out a sheet of photographs. *Please let me look cute. Please, please, please—*

"Oh, no," Jenna whispered, horrified, as she stared at the sheet. She was looking at what had to be the worst photograph taken in the history of middle school. In the history of the world! *I knew it was going to be awful!* she thought, thinking back to that day. Just as the portrait photographer had gotten ready to take her class picture, Jenna had remembered that she was still wearing her retainer. She had been using her tongue to push it out of her mouth when *flash!*

There was *no way* she was letting her mom give these out to people.

"Hey, Jenna!"

Jenna looked up. Her best friend, Matt, was coming toward her.

When he reached Jenna, Matt got behind her so that they were back to back. Then, out of nowhere, he pulled out a camera, aimed it at them, and clicked.

"Matt, please," Jenna said through gritted teeth. She should have seen it coming. Matt Flamhaff never went anywhere without a camera. "No more pictures."

"It's your thirteenth birthday," Matt said, grinning. A clump of dark brown hair fell over his forehead. "We've got to document it."

Just then, Jenna spotted Tom-Tom Rabideau and her five sidekicks—Brie, Julia, Meghan, Britney, and Sara—coming their way.

The Six Chicks.

The Six Chicks were everything Jenna wasn't. Extremely cool, extremely well dressed, and extremely snotty.

Jenna put on what she hoped was a cool but friendly smile. "Hi, Tom-Tom."

Tom-Tom gave her the once-over. "Hey, Jenna." Then her gaze swiveled to Matt. "Hi, Beaver. How's everything at the dam?"

Jenna winced. It was true that Matt had kind of a problem with his teeth, but making fun of him wasn't going to help. She pretended she didn't notice the remark—it wasn't any old day that Tom-Tom bothered to talk to her in the hallway. She needed to take full advantage of the opportunity.

"I don't know," Matt said sarcastically. "How's everything at the mall?"

Tom-Tom sniffed and turned back to Jenna. She tilted her head toward Jenna's photo packet. "How'd yours come out, Rink?"

"Not so good," Jenna admitted, holding the packet close to her chest just in case the Six Chicks tried to sneak a peek.

Tom-Tom sighed dramatically. "Yeah, mine aren't so hot either."

3

"Nuh-uh," Brie told her, vehemently shaking her head. "Yours are great, Tom-Tom."

"Yours are the best," Julia said loyally.

With a slightly embarrassed expression on her face, Tom-Tom pulled out a 5x7 from her own photo packet. Jenna gazed at it. Tom-Tom's blond hair was perfect, her snow-white teeth were straight and gleaming, and her eyes sparkled. "God, you're so photogenic!" Jenna blurted out.

Matt rolled his eyes. "I'll see you out front, okay, Jenna?"

"Do whatever you want," Tom-Tom told him, her voice dripping with condescension. "It's not like she needs a play-by-play." The Six Chicks all giggled, and after a second, Jenna giggled, too.

"Freakazoid," Tom-Tom muttered as Matt walked off. She leaned in close to Jenna. "FYI, I told Chris Grandy that me and the Six Chicks were going to come to your party tonight and he said he wanted to come with."

"Really?" Jenna said, her pulse quickening. Chris Grandy was only the cutest boy in the whole school. He had thick, wavy blond hair, beautiful eyes, and a great smile. Even better, he was the quarterback of the football team.

He was perfect.

Then Tom-Tom flipped her long hair over her shoulder. "Too bad we can't make it. Because we really wanted to. Didn't we, girls?"

"We totally did," Meghan said, nodding.

"So, so much," Britney and Sara trilled.

Jenna's smile slipped off her face.

"Ms. Measly is totally up our butts about our group project proposal and it's due tomorrow," Tom-Tom went on. "Since Chris is our really good friend, he's gonna come over to help us out, so I guess he can't go, either." She made a sad face.

"So you're *not* coming?" Jenna asked, disappointment welling up inside her. Her birthday party had been her one big chance to show the Six Chicks that she was just as cool as they were. Or at least, could be, if they'd let her be their friend.

Tom-Tom sighed. "Well, we can't all be brains like you." She took out a tube of lip gloss and slicked some on her lips, giving Jenna a helpless shrug.

"I could . . . write your report for you," Jenna offered, not wanting to lose the opportunity to have the coolest people at school at her party.

"You could?" Tom-Tom said, her eyes

5

wide. "Fabuloso!" She motioned to the chicks and they sauntered off down the hallway.

Jenna clutched her photo packet to her chest. She'd only been a teenager for a few hours, and already amazing things were happening.

Tonight was going to be the biggest night of her life.

● ● ●

"I can't believe you invited those clones," Matt said, shaking his head as he and Jenna walked home from school along Spruce Street.

"Be nice, Matt," Jenna chided him. "They're my friends."

He snorted. "The Six Chicks are *not* your friends."

"Well, almost," Jenna insisted, scuffing her shoe along the sidewalk. "And someday I'm going to *be* a Six Chick." She could imagine it now. Brie and Julia would be telling her how great she was, Britney and Sara would let her borrow anything from their amazing wardrobes, Meghan would save her a seat in the cafeteria, and Tom-Tom would ask her to—

"There's six of them, Jenna," Matt said, interrupting her thoughts. "That's the whole point. You can't be the seventh Six Chick. It's mathematically impossible. Besides, you're way better than them. They're totally unoriginal."

"And totally popular," Jenna said enviously. The Six Chicks were everything she wanted to be. They were popular, they had style, and they would always be completely fabuloso.

"I don't want to be original, Matt," she admitted. "I want to be cool."

They stopped in front of their side-by-side houses, and Matt took a package of candy from his pants pocket. "You want some Razzles?"

"I'm thirteen today, Mr. Flamhaff," Jenna said, putting on her best grown-up voice. "I'm too old for Razzles. Razzles are for kids."

"Exactly," Matt said. With a grin, Jenna held out her cupped hand and Matt poured some Razzles into it. He poured some for himself, and together they tilted their heads back and dumped the Razzles into their mouths. Tart, sweet candy—and then gum. Perfect.

"Well . . . *arrivederci!*" Matt said.

They had a tradition of saying goodbye by

using foreign words. The Romance languages were Jenna's favorites.

"Au revoir," Jenna said. Then she ran up the sidewalk to her house. She had a party to get ready for.

● ● ● **two**

Jenna's heart was beating double-time as she sat in front of her bedroom vanity. Her thirteenth-birthday party was almost about to begin, and she looked awesome! She had on a snug aqua-colored top trimmed with jewels, a white belt, tasseled boots, and new star-shaped birthday earrings, and her hair was teased as big as she had ever made it.

A rock video was ending on her small TV. A model with long hair and really big breasts was flouncing around, hanging all over the guitar player. Frowning, Jenna looked into her oval mirror once more and compared her own chest to the model's.

There *was* no comparison.

Will they ever grow? Jenna thought, frustrated. Impulsively she grabbed her tissue box and stuffed a few fistfuls of tissues into her bra. Much better. "We are young, heartache to heartache . . ." Holding her eyeliner wand a few inches from her face, Jenna glanced over at the new video. Pat Benatar, in a shredded-looking outfit, was dancing with a bunch of people.

She is so cool, Jenna thought enviously, admiring Pat's choreographed MTV moves. *And she has great cheekbones.*

Jenna stared back at her reflection. She would never make it as a video star, that was for sure, but she looked pretty good—almost as good as the models in *Poise,* the bible of all things cool. Jenna had plastered every inch of her room with ripped-out pages from the magazine. The models inside were *so* perfect. Jenna was sure they had never had to go to school with a zit or have their mother still want to pick out their clothes.

Or take the world's most mortifying school photo.

Then a new video came on, and Jenna whipped her head around as the opening notes played.

It was Him.

The cutest, most talented rock star in the world.

Rick Springfield.

Suddenly her bedroom door burst open. "Happy birthday, Jenna!" boomed her parents' voices from the doorway.

"Aggh!" Flustered, Jenna spun around. *Don't closed doors mean anything anymore?* she thought, staring with dismay at the huge video camera in her father's hands. A camera that was trained on her. "Don't you ever knock?"

"Come on, birthday girl," her father said from behind the camera. "Tell us all about your new life as a teenager!"

Jenna quickly crossed her arms across her chest in an attempt to hide her new, improved bra size. "Could you guys just leave? Please?"

Her father put the camera aside and stared in shock at Jenna's chest.

"Honey, what did you do?" her mother said, putting her hand to her mouth.

Jenna dove onto her bed, landing on a pile of old issues of *Poise*. "Go away!" she shouted, her voice muffled by her bedspread.

Her mother shooed her father out, then

11

turned back to Jenna. Feeling totally humiliated, Jenna stood there as her mother removed
tissue after tissue from her bra.

"It's going to be okay, Jenna," her mom
said softly.

"It is not, Mom!" Jenna cried. "Look at
me!" She pointed to her flat chest. "This is not
okay. This is fatal!"

Her mom smiled. "No, it's realistic." She
moistened one of the tissues with her tongue
and began to wipe off some of Jenna's makeup.

I feel like a cat having a bath, Jenna
thought morosely. She grabbed a nearby issue
of *Poise* and began flipping through its pages.
"I hate my life."

Her mom smoothed her hair back. "Just
because you don't look like one of the girls in
Poise magazine doesn't mean you're not beautiful in your own way."

"I don't want to be beautiful in my own way!"
Jenna cried. She stabbed her finger at one of the
photo spreads. "I want to look like these people!"

"These are not people, honey," her
mother said. "They're models."

"'Thirty, flirty, and thriving: why the thirties
are the best years of your life,'" Jenna read aloud.

She turned the page. "Oh my God. Look at her apartment!" A gorgeous model lounged on a sleek leather couch. Huge floor-to-ceiling windows gazed out on New York City. "I want to be thirty," Jenna muttered. She couldn't wait to be a grown-up—all her problems would be over.

"Oh, you will be, honey. Sooner than you think." Her mother stood back and surveyed Jenna's newly cleansed face. "That's more like it."

Jenna looked into the mirror and was horrified to see who was looking back at her: plain old Jenna Rink.

The moment her mother was out of the room, Jenna snatched up the tissue box and began restuffing her bra.

Her mom was nice, but she didn't know anything about being a girl.

● ● ●

"'Cause this is Thriller,'" Jenna sang to herself as she mimicked the moves from the Michael Jackson video that was playing on the basement television. Her parents had transformed their rec room into a disco—there was even a glittery silver disco ball hanging from the

13

ceiling. A light machine swirled lights around the room. Jenna had to admit, it looked pretty good. Pretty soon everyone would be at her house.

Pretty soon *Chris Grandy* would be at her house!

Suddenly Jenna noticed Matt standing on the basement stairs. He was holding a very large gift-wrapped box.

"Oh, my God, Matt!" Jenna said, stopping her dancing. "That's like the biggest gift ever!"

"This is just part one of your present," Matt said, looking pleased. "I've got something else to give you later."

Jenna shut off the music as Matt set the box down and lifted the top off. Inside was a large pink dollhouse.

"Happy birthday!" Matt shouted.

Jenna knelt down to get a closer look at it. "You made all this?" she asked, taken aback.

"Yeah. You know how you were always asking for a Barbie Dream House but your parents never got it for you?"

"Uh-huh," Jenna said slowly.

"Well, I figured now that you're thirteen, you've way outgrown that, so I decided to make you your own custom dream house. This is a Jenna Dream House!" He opened up the house to reveal a master bedroom that was decorated with mini-cutouts of Jenna's favorite singers, actresses, and stuffed animals. And there were dolls—with Jenna's picture taped to their heads!

"Here's you in your bedroom with a massive stereo and every record ever made. The good ones, I mean," Matt said excitedly. "And here you are in a bubble bath, reading your favorite magazine. This is your art room where you make your collages. That bum loafing on the couch is your friend, Rick Springfield." Matt pointed to a small photograph. "And that's me, making sure the creep keeps his hands to himself." Jenna saw that Matt had glued a photo of his own face, wearing an angry expression, on a tiny figurine.

Jenna laughed. This was incredible.

"I almost forgot." Matt pulled out an orange paper packet with yellow letters that read WISHING DUST. "I ordered it off the back of last month's *Hulk*." He squinted at the label. "'This wishing dust knows what's in your heart of hearts. It will make all your dreams come true.'" Jenna watched as Matt sprinkled the dust over the Dream House. Glittery pink and yellow crystals landed gently on the rooftop.

What would it be like to have all your wishes come true? Jenna wondered, transfixed.

"If I forgot anything or if you want me to add something, I could," Matt said, his face serious. "No problem."

"Let's see," Jenna mused, enjoying the fantasy. "Could you make it more of, like, a Fifth Avenue apartment with a huge closet *full* of all the best clothes? And a giant bathroom with every kind of makeup that I get for free because all the companies know that if *Jenna Rink* wears their makeup, then everyone will want to."

"But—"

Ding-dong!

"Oh, my God!" Jenna shrieked. Someone was here! "Um, Matt, I'm just going to put this away, okay? So there's room to dance." *What if Chris saw it and thought I still played with dolls? Worse yet, what if Tom-Tom saw it?* She picked up the house, stuck it on a shelf in the closet, and slammed the door.

Then she dashed upstairs. "Put some music on!" she shouted back to Matt.

"Dad!" she shrieked as her father went to

open the front door. "You promised you were going to stay upstairs!"

Her father threw his hands up and walked out of the foyer.

Taking a deep breath, Jenna opened the door. And there, on her front steps, stood Tom-Tom and the rest of the Six Chicks.

"Hi, guys! Come in!" Jenna said eagerly, stepping to the side. "Um . . . the party's downstairs. Fabuloso!"

She blinked as each of the chicks filed past her, each girl handing her a jacket. Pretty soon the jackets were piled up all the way to her chin. She was just about to push the front door closed when—

Vroom! A souped-up Camaro pulled up in front of the house, the Eurythmics' "Sweet Dreams" blasting from the stereo. Jenna stared, frozen, as Chris Grandy stepped out of the front seat, giving his feathered hair an expert flip. Two of his friends climbed out of the back, and the car peeled off.

He came!

● ● ●

Jenna's party wasn't getting off to the smoothest start. First of all, she wasn't really sure what sorts of things really cool people did at parties. There were a few boys standing over by her paneled basement wall, looking kind of uncomfortable. Tom-Tom and the Six Chicks kept whispering and giggling to each other. And Chris Grandy and his friends slouched over by a table of mini hot dogs, not saying anything.

This is awful! Jenna thought, her whole body going tense. *What am I going to do?*

To make matters worse, Matt was standing next to Jenna's boom box, bobbing his head up and down to the Talking Heads. The only reason Jenna knew who it was, was because he was always going on and on about bands normal people never had heard of. From the looks of things, he was the only fan in the room.

"What is this?" Tom-Tom asked Jenna, wrinkling up her nose as if she was smelling something putrid.

Jenna mustered a smile. "I'm not sure—it's Matt's," she said, shrugging.

With a determined look on her face, Tom-Tom strode across the room and clicked off the boom box. The rec room was totally silent.

"Sorry, Beav-head, majority rules," she said, giving Matt a cold smirk. Tom-Tom popped the cassette out and handed it over to Matt.

A few people laughed.

"Narrow, man," Matt said, shaking his head. "Narrow, hopeless people." He walked over to Jenna. "I need to go next door and get my guitar."

"Do whatever you want, Matt," Jenna said, knowing that the Six Chicks were watching. She tried to sound bored. *I bet Chris Grandy doesn't spend his spare time listening to music like this.* "It's not like I need a play-by-play."

The other girls giggled, and Jenna felt her shoulders relax. Maybe she had a chance with the popular crowd after all.

She tried to ignore the hurt look on Matt's face as he turned and went upstairs. *I mean, it's not like I'm not going to talk to him. It's just—*

"Hey, you guys, I have an idea," Tom-Tom said. "Let's play Seven Minutes in Heaven."

One of Chris's friends hooted.

"Yeah," Jenna said, pretending to know what Tom-Tom was talking about. "Um, how does that one go again?"

Tom-Tom flashed her a big smile. "You go first 'cause you're the birthday girl." She took a scarf from around her neck and used it to blindfold Jenna.

"Now what?" Jenna asked, trying not to sound nervous.

Tom-Tom put her hands on Jenna's shoulders and pushed her. "Now you go in the closet and some lucky guy is going to meet you in there and do whatever he wants with you for seven whole minutes."

Jenna could feel the blood whoosh from her cheeks.

"Guess who wants to go first?" Tom-Tom whispered in her ear.

"Who?" Jenna whispered back, her heart hammering.

"Chris Grandy."

Jenna felt goose bumps break out along her arms. "No way."

She could feel Tom-Tom's breath as the ringleader of the Six Chicks leaned closer. "Way." Tom-Tom steered Jenna inside the closet. "Oh. Before I forget," Tom-Tom said. "Where's our project proposal?"

"By the stereo," Jenna said.

"Thanks," Tom-Tom said. Then she lowered her voice. "Remember, no peeking. Keep that blindfold on. And just so you know? Chris *loves* going for second base."

Tom-Tom slammed the closet door. Quickly, Jenna began pulling the tissue out of her bra. There was no way she wanted Chris Grandy to go for second base and find out that her curvy figure was fake!

Jenna sat down and waited, wishing she could take the blindfold off. She fluffed her hair with her fingers and gave her hand a few fast practice kisses.

Come on, Chris, please, she thought, wondering what was taking so long. Shouldn't he be coming in by now? Jenna didn't even hear anyone talking.

Then she heard the closet door slowly open. "I thought you weren't gonna come," Jenna said, relief and nerves flooding through her. "Where are you?" She reached out and felt around in the air.

Chris held up his hand and laced his fingers with her.

"Oh," Jenna said, her heart in her throat. Swallowing, she lifted up her face, waiting for Chris to kiss her. She could feel his breath, warm on her cheeks. "Oh, Chris," she whispered.

And then a voice that she had heard every day of her life—a voice she absolutely did not want to hear now—said, "It's not Chris. It's . . . Matt."

Jenna yanked off her blindfold, blinking fast. There, sitting in front of her, the lights from the disco ball spilling onto his chubby face, was Matt! "What are you doing here?" she cried, mortified.

All Matt did was gape at her. No words came out of his mouth.

"Where's Chris?" Jenna asked, peering past Matt into the rec room.

"He's gone," Matt said finally. "Everybody left."

Jenna stood up and stormed out of the closet. That couldn't be true! But as she gazed around the empty basement, she realized it was. She spun on her heel to face Matt.

"What did you do?"

"Nothing," Matt said unhappily.

"Yes you did!" Jenna shouted. He had to have done something—something that had scared everyone at her party away!

"No I didn't," Matt insisted, his dark eyes wide. "I just came over to play you your song. For your birthday." He pointed toward an electric guitar and a small portable amplifier that sat on the floor.

"Get out!" Jenna cried, feeling tears pool in her eyes.

Matt looked miserable. "Jenna, please."

But Jenna *felt* miserable. "Get out!" She pulled him from the closet, got inside, and slammed the door. Her hands were shaking.

"Jenna." Matt's voice came from outside. "Let me talk to you."

"No!" Jenna said. She had never felt so humiliated in her life. "I hate you. I hate me. I hate everybody!" She pulled the blindfold back over her eyes. *I wish I could disappear.* She began to rock back and forth.

A tear ran down her cheek. *The Six Chicks left me here. This was all just a big joke.* "What was I thinking?" Jenna croaked out. Chris Grandy wasn't coming in to play Seven Minutes in Heaven. No one was. No one but Matt.

"Come on, Jenna. It's your birthday," Matt pleaded.

"I don't want to be thirteen!" Jenna cried. More tears slid out from underneath the blindfold. "I want to be thirty! Thirty, flirty, and thriving."

"What?"

She shoved herself back against the closet wall as Matt began strumming his guitar.

Jenna covered her ears to block out Matt's electric serenade. "Thirty and flirty and thriving," she whispered, her voice catching. "Thirty and flirty and thriving." She repeated the phrase again. And again.

Above her, the Dream House teetered precariously on the edge of the closet shelf. What Jenna didn't see was that some of Matt's wishing dust had spilled out, sprinkling tiny grains of sand onto Jenna's hair.

Then some wishing dust landed in her tears.

And when wishing dust mixes with the tears of a thirteen-year-old girl making a wish . . . anything can happen.

Especially the wish.

● ● ● three

The first thing Jenna noticed when she woke up the next morning was that she couldn't see. Everything was completely, 100 percent black. And it was eerily quiet. No crickets, no garbage trucks rumbling past the house, no whistling teakettles—nothing. Nothing except something really loud and annoying blasting from her clock radio. She smacked her hand on the snooze button, shutting it off.

Even her sheets felt weird, all slippery and cold instead of her usual warm flannel ones. "Ow!" Jenna yelped as she got out of bed and promptly stubbed her toe. Who had moved her nightstand? "Shoot!" she said as she stumbled into what she thought was her bookshelf. It was so dark in the room, she couldn't see a thing. Not only was the world dark, but she didn't even remember going to bed the night before.

When she got to her bedroom doorway, she tried without success to find the doorknob. Her hands felt nothing but air.

Jenna reached up to touch her eyes. There was something over them. *I'm wearing a sleep mask!* That explained it. Well, sort of. She took the mask off.

"Mom?" Jenna said warily, blinking in the sudden brightness. "Dad?"

No one answered her.

She was in a living room, but it wasn't her parents'. This room was much fancier, and the furniture all looked brand-new and very modern. There was something familiar about it, but Jenna couldn't quite place it.

Where am I?

She spied an uncorked bottle of wine on

top of a cabinet. "The punch! Chris Grandy must have spiked the punch!" she said, trying to convince herself that that was what had happened. "This is normal, Jenna, this is what happens when you get drunk," she said firmly.

But she didn't have a headache or feel sick, the way people on TV who drank too much did. "No, no, I'm dreaming," she said, pacing the room. "This is a really weird dream." There was a desk behind her, with a phone on top. She walked over to it, picked it up, and dialed her home number.

"Hi, sorry we've missed your call," came her dad's voice on the answering machine. Answering machine—when did her parents get that? "Well, not that sorry, because we're cruising in the Caribbean! We'll be back on the eighteenth, so call us then!" *Beeeeeep*.

"You went on a cruise without me?" Jenna cried out in disbelief. Next to the phone was a pile of bills. She picked one up. It was addressed to Jenna Rink.

"Jenna Rink!" Jenna sat down on a gold leather chair and flipped quickly through the pile. They were all addressed to her! "Jenna Rink, Jenna Rink, Jenna Rink . . . oh my God. *I live here*."

This place! Jenna realized, looking around her once more. Now she realized what was familiar. It looked exactly like the photo of the apartment in *Poise*—right down to the glass coffee table with a fruit bowl on it!

"Okay, okay, stay calm," Jenna told herself, cautiously making her way down an unfamiliar hallway. What she needed was a drink of water. Or a good cold splash on her face. Something to help snap her to her senses.

As she passed a hall mirror, she stopped in her tracks. She could feel the blood rushing from her face, pooling in her toes. She wasn't alone.

"Oh! You scared me," she said, turning to the woman who was standing behind her. But . . . the woman was gone! Jenna turned back to the mirror. There was the woman again. Tall, with straight shoulder-length brown hair, brown eyes, and full red lips, wearing a watermelon-pink slip trimmed with black lace.

Jenna lifted her hand—and the woman lifted hers, too. *Wait a second.* . . . Jenna touched her face. The woman touched her own face. Jenna looked into a mirror on the side and saw that she had—breasts! Real ones! With a shaking hand, Jenna touched her chest.

They're real! Then she stared into the mirror.

"Ahhhhhh!" she screamed. And so did the woman. "What is happening?" Jenna squeaked. But she already knew. There wasn't another woman.

That beautiful almost-thirty-year-old woman was—her!

Oh my God.

Jenna reached up and touched her face, and then stared down at her long legs and her full chest. This apartment, this body . . . *I'm thirty, flirty, and . . . thriving,* she thought, weak in the knees.

And then Jenna heard a sound.

The sound of water running in a shower.

I'm not alone, she thought, petrified. She ran over and grabbed a red umbrella from a stand in the apartment's foyer and crept back down the hall toward the bathroom. "Okay, I know you're in there!" she yelled, trying to sound tough. "And my parents are totally coming home any minute!"

Jenna stood in front of the bathroom door, her knees shaking. *Whoosh!* The door swung open. Standing in front of her was a guy who looked about twenty-five, wearing a towel around his waist—and nothing else!

Startled, Jenna accidentally squeezed the umbrella mechanism, popping it open.

"Hey, Sweetbottom," the guy said, giving her a lazy smile. "You seen my conditioner?"

"Oh my God!" Jenna shrieked, turning away and then turning back again. "You're naked!"

The guy smiled again and winked. "Not yet." To her horror, he pulled the towel from his waist, giving her a full view before she could avert her eyes.

"Eek!" Jenna squeaked, throwing the umbrella at him and running down the hallway.

"You wanna join me?" the guy called out.

Was he crazy? Jenna grabbed a polka-dotted coat, an expensive-looking leather purse, and the nearest pair of shoes.

Then she ran out the door.

● ● ●

When she got to the street, Jenna had no idea what to do or where to go. The sun was shining, taxicabs were honking, and there were busy-looking people walking everywhere.

I'm not in New Jersey. I'm in the city, Jenna

realized, staring up at the tall buildings that surrounded her. *New York City!*

Swallowing, she started to walk up the street. A tinkling of music caught her ear. Where was it coming from?

"Can you hear it, too?" Jenna asked a woman walking past her. But the woman looked at her as if she was crazy and kept right on walking.

"Jenna!"

Jenna turned. A sophisticated-looking young blond woman wearing a short silvery-blue jacket was leaning against a fancy black car, holding a cup of coffee in one hand and what looked like a calculator in the other.

"Could you hurry up just a little bit?" the woman said impatiently to her. Then she held the calculator to her ear. "I don't care if you have to drag Justin by his testicles, just make sure he's at our party. He made a com-*mit*-ment." She turned back to Jenna again. "Let's go! We're late."

"I don't get in cars with strangers," Jenna replied nervously, staring at the calculator. *That's a phone!* she realized.

The woman put her hand over the phone.

"Did you drink kamikazes last night? You know tequila makes you paranoid." Then she put the phone to her lips once more. "He had my number," she snarled. "Just tell him that Lucy Wyman called and he's got twelve hours to get his butt back to New York."

"Jenna! Baby!"

She looked up. The guy from the apartment was hanging out of a window. "Don't make me come down there and grab you." Then he made a growling noise. "Rowr!"

Pushing her mother's warnings out of her mind, Jenna leapt into the car.

"Honey, as your best friend, I gotta tell you something," Lucy said, patting Jenna's knee as the driver of the car pulled out into traffic. "The slip dress thing is totally 1997." A tense look spread across her face. "Unless—is it retro already?"

1997? Jenna bit her lip. "Um . . . Lucy?" She paused. "Are we really best friends?" There was something familiar about the woman, but Jenna couldn't figure out what it was.

Lucy studied her. She nodded, a look of recognition spreading across her face. "You're pregnant, aren't you?"

"What?" Jenna shrieked. "Oh my God! No!"

"What, then?" Lucy demanded, sinking back in her black leather seat. "God, you scared me. What *did* you do last night?"

"That's the problem!" Jenna burst out. "Something really strange is happening to me! I slept in an apartment I've never seen before, I found some naked man in the shower this morning—I saw his thingy!" She closed her eyes, shuddering. It was so gross!

"Oh, God, his thingy. Was it that bad?" Lucy signaled to the driver. "Far corner, please."

Lucy hopped out and began striding down the sidewalk. Jenna followed suit, trying to keep up in her heels. A street sign said 6th Avenue.

"Lucy, please listen to me. I'm *thirteen*."

Instead of the helpful reaction Jenna had hoped for, Lucy snorted. "If you're gonna start lying about your age, I'd go with twenty-seven."

"No, I know it's strange, but, like, some really weird dream happened and—" Jenna cut herself off as the music began to play again. "Like that! Can you hear it? It keeps *following me*!"

"Would you stop being ridiculous?" Lucy snapped. "It's probably Richard."

"Who's Richard?" Jenna asked, bewildered.

Lucy gave an exasperated snort. "Richard is

your boss . . . ? You know, British guy? Curly hair?" Lucy stuck her hand into Jenna's purse and pulled out a tiny phone, just like the one she had been using. She pressed a button and thrust it at Jenna.

"H-hello?" Jenna stammered. Then her eyes narrowed as she listened to the voice on the other end. It was the guy from the apartment! "You! *You* put on your pants and stop calling me Sweetbottom!" She frantically pushed all the buttons on the phone, trying to hang it up.

"Who was that?" Lucy asked, her eyes wide.

"I don't know his name!" Jenna said, on the verge of full-blown hysteria. "I don't know what's happening. I don't know what to do!"

Lucy grabbed her by the shoulders. "Jenna. Stop! I'm going to tell you exactly what you're going to do. Okay?"

Jenna nodded, hoping she wouldn't start to cry. "Mmm-hmm."

"I want you to repeat after me: 'I am Jenna Rink, big-time magazine editor.'"

Jenna gaped at her. "I am?"

"Repeat it!"

"I am Jenna Rink, big-time magazine editor?"

Lucy continued. "'I'm a tough bitch.'"

Jenna blinked. This grown-up was telling her to swear?

"Say it!" Lucy barked.

Mom, forgive me, okay? Jenna repeated, "I'm a tough . . . bitch."

"'I'm gonna walk in and not let anyone know I'm hung over—'"

"I'm not!" Jenna protested.

Lucy planted her hands on her hips.

With a sigh, Jenna repeated, "I'm gonna walk in and not let anyone know I'm hung over. . . ."

"'Because the future of *Poise* depends on me,'" Lucy finished.

"Poise?" Jenna repeated dumbly. That was her favorite magazine. The bible. Anyone who was cool read *Poise.*

Lucy glared at her, then pointed above them. POISE. The letters hung above a revolving glass door that led into a sleek-looking skyscraper.

I—I work here? Jenna thought, the idea hitting her like a ton of bricks. Lucy pushed through the revolving door, and Jenna followed. *I—I work here!*

Lucy didn't say another word as the elevator took them up to the fifteenth floor. She got off and walked briskly down the hall. Jenna wobbled behind her—and fell smack on her face. Scrambling to her feet, she did her best to catch up.

"Good morning, Ms. Rink, good morning, Ms. Wyman," said a curly-haired middle-aged woman sitting at a desk near the entrance.

"Good morning . . . ," Jenna said politely. "Um, what's her name?" she whispered to Lucy.

"Who cares?" Lucy said, not breaking her stride. More people said hello and smiled, and Jenna tried to smile at each of them. They all seemed to know her by name.

What was weird was that they all seemed nervous around her.

Finally they stopped near a door and Jenna noticed that the nameplate alongside it said JENNA RINK. *Cool!* she thought, excited for a moment.

A harried-looking bald guy came over, a worried expression on his face. "Jenna, please, don't yell at me because it's not my fault, but they came in late from the printer and they need a decision now." He held up two different posters featuring people at a party.

Jenna stood there, uncertain, and Lucy poked her in the ribs. "Just pick one."

Jenna pointed. "That one?"

The bald man beamed. "Love it! Knew it! Genius!" He scurried away.

The woman who had first greeted them reappeared. "Eminem's on the phone and wants a decision *now*."

Jenna's face lit up. "M&M's? Plain. No, peanut. No, plain! Ouch!" she complained as Lucy yanked her arm and pulled her down the hallway.

A thin, athletic-looking man with super-gelled hair and a narrow goatee, and wearing a tight black sweater and pants, came over.

"There's the dynamic duo!" he boomed in a British accent. "I trust my executive editors are late again because they were out promoting us at all the right parties?"

Lucy smiled. "You got it, Richard."

"Richard?" Jenna said, making the connection. "You're my boss!"

Richard grinned. "That's right, baby. Who's your daddy?"

"Wayne Rink," Jenna told him, furrowing her brow.

For some reason, Richard thought this was funny. "You slay me, Jenna, and the look—*wowza*. A sort of Rita Hayworth meets Dorothy, bed-heady thing. I love." He turned to the young woman hovering beside him. "Make a note of it, it's fabulous." And with that, Richard threw open the door of what appeared to be a large conference room.

Jenna drank it all in. There stood people she guessed were editors, chitchatting about parties and clothes and celebrity gossip.

The curly-haired woman came over and handed Jenna a cup of coffee and a scone. "Is there anything else you need from me, Jenna?"

Jenna had heard someone call the woman Arlene. "You mean, like a favor?" she asked, taking a small nibble of scone.

Arlene hesitated. "Sure, like a favor."

"I need to find this guy," Jenna whispered. She had to find Matt! Maybe he could tell her what had happened, or help her figure out what to do!

Arlene nodded slightly. "Never a problem, Jenna."

"I have his phone number," Jenna told her. Richard stuck his head between them.

"Arlene, leave us, please." To Jenna's dismay, Arlene hurried out.

Jenna grabbed a piece of paper and wrote *Matt Flamhaff, (201) 555-0139.*

"Jenna, sweetheart," said a thin woman from across the room, "are we going for a look or did we get dressed *before* we showered this morning?"

Giving her a small smile, Jenna scrunched up the paper into a ball and threw it toward Arlene, hitting her on the back.

Everyone in the room looked at Jenna as if she had lost her mind. *Well, maybe I have!* Jenna thought, gazing down at her new body. She stretched and pretended to yawn, watching as Arlene picked up the paper and left.

"Jenna's hung over," Lucy stage-whispered to the room. "The big three-oh looms."

"Ohhhh," everyone in the room said knowingly as they took their seats.

Jenna's eyes followed Richard as he stood and held up a copy of *Sparkle* magazine. It was another fashion magazine, but *Sparkle*'s stories were never as good as the ones in *Poise,* Jenna knew. On the *Sparkle* cover it said, "J.Lo's Eleventh Secret: Shhh! The One She Wouldn't Tell!"

"Okay," Richard said. "You've seen this, of course." He ripped off the cover and pinned it on a wall next to a cover from *Poise* that read, "Jennifer Lopez: Her Ten Big Secrets."

"Hmmm," Richard said, scratching his chin. "I wonder which one Holly Housewife's going to grab at the local supermarket."

Jenna wondered, too. Who was Jennifer Lopez?

For the first time Jenna noticed that the walls of the conference room were plastered with covers of *Poise* and *Sparkle*, the competing issues side by side. The January *Poise* was next to the January *Sparkle*, the February *Poise* was next to the February *Sparkle*, and so on.

And month after month, it appeared that *Sparkle* had something better than *Poise*.

I guess other things have changed, too, Jenna thought, sad to see her favorite magazine coming in second.

"Seven months in a row now they scoop us?" Richard ranted. "It's like they have *Sparkle* cams hidden in our walls!" He stared at some of the magazine covers as if there were hidden cameras behind them. "You watching? Are you watching me? Hello . . . hello." Then he did something that made Jenna gasp. He gave them a double middle-finger salute! "Why don't you sparkle this, you cheap, slimy copycats!"

Jenna snorted back a giggle. Now, that was a putdown! "Sparkle this!" she repeated.

"Richard, we're hiring new printers, we're creating new passwords and putting up fire-walls on all our computers," Lucy said calmly. "Jenna fired Charlotte yesterday."

"You did?" Richard asked, turning to her.

Jenna didn't know what to say. She didn't even know who Charlotte was!

"Good!" Richard said. "I *guarantee* you she has friends at *Sparkle*. She was always tak-ing notes."

Lucy rolled her eyes. "She was a *secretary*."

Richard waved her comment away. "Whatever. Our party tonight is now huge. We need to make an unequivocal statement that *Poise* is still hot and happening."

"Got it," Lucy said briskly.

"Now, we need a newsstand circ analysis done immediately. I also strongly suggest we take apart our F.O.B., overhaul the B.O.B, think about new heads, decks, and slugs."

He sucked in air. "Jenna, what do you think?"

Think? Jenna didn't know what to think. She might be an executive editor (!) but she hadn't understood one word Richard had said. So she raised her hand. "Um . . . can I go to the bathroom?"

● ● ● four

While everyone in the conference room continued to talk about F.O.B.'s and B.O.B's, and J.Lo, Jenna sneaked back to her office. Closing the door behind her, she leaned against it with her eyes shut, trying to catch her breath.

Okay. Let me get this straight. According to the date printed on the magazines, it's 2004—not 1987. I have a cool apartment and I work at Poise *magazine.*

I am a grown-up. I'm thirty, flirty, and . . . thriving, she thought, weak in the knees.

Her wish had come true!

Then she opened her eyes. *This is really my office!* she thought, gazing around in awe. There was a framed diploma on the wall. "I got a Bachelor of Arts in communications," she whispered, touching the glass with her fingertip. "Wow." And what a view! The people down on the street looked like ants from up here. One of the walls had shelves, and there were tons of framed photographs. There was Jenna—the grown-up Jenna—dancing with Lucy; then standing next to a man with brown hair; then standing next to a man with blond hair; and in a third picture, standing with the man from the shower! "It's the naked guy!" Jenna whispered, stunned. *Is he my boyfriend?* Thank heavens he had clothes on.

Then Jenna gasped. There was a picture of her with Madonna! Scrawled across the photograph in black ink were the words *Jenna girl, margaritas anytime! Love ya, Madonna.*

"I'm friends with Madonna?" Jenna said, stunned. *We drink margaritas together?*

Things were even more awesome than she had ever imagined.

Someone knocked at the door. Jenna

hesitated, then opened the door a teeny tiny bit. It was Arlene.

"Here are your messages," Arlene said, giving her a stack of small papers. "And this morning, your mother called from Barbados—"

"My mom?" Jenna said, dismayed. "Why didn't you tell me?"

"I'm sorry, Ms. Rink," Arlene said, looking confused. "I thought you said never to bother you with family calls."

"I did?" Jenna asked, surprised. That sounded so—so mean!

"Please don't fire me," Arlene begged.

"No, no, it's . . . it's okay," Jenna said, thinking fast. "I forgot I said that before . . . um, just please tell me next time she calls, okay?"

Arlene nodded. "Yes, ma'am." She cleared her throat. "And I have that information you asked for."

"Matt!" Jenna shouted, throwing open the door and pulling Arlene inside.

"The phone number you gave me belongs to his parents. I told them I was calling from Visa and that he was in a lot of trouble."

"You lied?" Jenna asked, her eyes wide.

The adults in this place sure did some questionable things.

Arlene handed her another slip of paper. "Two twelve Perry Street. It's in the Village."

"What village?" Jenna asked, hoping Matt hadn't moved somewhere really far away. *Please, God, don't let him be in Italy. Or Africa. Or—*

"Greenwich Village?" Arlene said, arching an eyebrow. "Downtown?"

"Oh, right, cool, cool," Jenna bluffed. "Greenwich Village."

A few moments later Jenna stood outside *Poise*'s front door, clutching Matt's address. She knew Greenwich Village was part of New York City, but where exactly it was, or how to get there, was a mystery.

So was hailing a cab. None of them would stop! "Excuse me?" she called out as one whizzed past her. She tried waving. Yoo-hooing. Raising her eyebrows as Arlene had done. Nothing worked.

So then, not knowing what else to do, she started to walk.

After what seemed like an eternity, she came to a run-down building with a rickety old fire escape. She looked at the paper, then at the building. *Yup, this is it*. She walked up and saw that there was a little directory of names next to the door. FLAMHAFF, 2B, said one. She pressed the button next to it, and a buzzer went off inside.

"Yeah?" came a male voice.

Jenna gulped. "Um, hi, this is Jenna, and I'm trying to find Matt. And I don't know if you're the right Matt, but if you used to live on Spruce Street and your favorite shirt is that blue velour one, then I really need to talk to you."

There was a moment of silence. Then, "Okay, I heard none of that. Let's try it this way. Ring two times if you're from Ming Gardens and you're here to surprise me with some egg rolls. If not, please go away."

Jenna thought for a second, then hit the buzzer twice. The door buzzed open.

Slowly, Jenna climbed the stairs. *Why didn't I grab a pair of sneakers?* she thought, wincing with each high-heeled step. There it was. 2B. She knocked. The door opened a few inches. A tall dark-haired guy, wearing jeans and a rumpled shirt, stood there.

"You're not Chinese," the guy said, peering over the security chain.

Jenna stared at him, trying to find her friend in that grown-up face. "Matt?" she said.

"Yeah?"

"Wow . . . you're tall, and, um, *different*."

"Uh-huh. Thanks. Do I know you?"

How could he not recognize me? I mean, I know I look grown-up, but still . . . "You don't know me?" A wave of sadness came over her. "But yesterday you were there. Well, um, not really yesterday, I guess, because I'm not thirteen right now—"

"Jenna?" Matt said slowly.

"Yes!" Jenna jumped in the air. "Matt! It's me, it's me, it's me!"

"Jenna Rink." Suddenly the door slammed. *But* . . .

The door opened wide. "Hey," Matt said.

She threw her arms around him in a huge hug. "Matt!"

● ● ●

Inside the tiny apartment Matt had a ton of stuff. There were cameras and crates and photographs and lots and lots of other things.

"And you still take pictures?" Jenna asked.

"Yeah. Pays the bills." Matt frowned. "Look, Jenna, I'm sorry, but . . . why are you here?"

Jenna groaned. "Matt, I told you, there's something really weird going on! Yesterday was my thirteenth birthday, and today I'm . . . I'm"—she pointed to herself—"this! And you, I mean, you're . . . that!" Matt was the same age as her. Tall! With grown-up clothes. And his own apartment!

Matt slumped into a chair. "Are you high?"

High? Jenna had no clue what he meant.

"Drugs, Jenna," Matt went on, cocking an eyebrow. "Pot, X—"

"Drugs?" Jenna shook her head vehemently. "No! I was in the closet, and I got bonked on the head, and I—I—I skipped everything! It's like a dream, Matt! I don't remember my life! You have to help me remember!"

Matt just stared at her as if she was crazy. "I don't think I can, Jenna."

"But why?"

He shrugged. "Well, I'm not really qualified. I don't know anything about you. I haven't seen you since high school."

Jenna couldn't believe what he was saying. "What?"

Matt sighed. "I'm sorry, Jenna, but . . . we're not really friends anymore."

Jenna could feel her mouth go dry and the back of her throat start to close up. Suddenly she was hot. Very hot. Her heart was racing, her knees felt like Jell-O, and a thin line of sweat was forming above her lip. Matt was her lifeline to the past. The only one who could help her. And . . . and he couldn't.

"Is it hot in here?" Jenna asked, fanning herself. "I think I need some air, some water, and a really fluffy pillow. Please?"

Matt didn't move. He just stared at her.

"I want a fluffy pillow!" she shouted.

And Matt flew to get one.

● ● ●

Jenna sat on a plastic chair on Matt's rooftop balcony, her arms wrapped tightly around her pillow. "Thank you," she said when Matt came outside and handed her a glass of water.

She gulped it down.

"Are you okay?" Matt asked.

Jenna stared out at the garden below. She didn't feel at all okay. "I'm scared," she said in a tiny voice, looking up at her friend. Or at least, the person who *used* to be her friend.

"This is all so freaky," Jenna said as they walked outside Matt's apartment. "It was just like yesterday we were walking to school." She took a deep breath. "I really haven't seen you? Ever?"

"No," Matt said, scuffing his toe on the sidewalk.

"But why?" Jenna asked. She couldn't understand it. She and Matt were going to be friends forever. They had an unspoken pact.

"Well, things got a little—you were just—hard to see," Matt said, shrugging.

A lump formed in Jenna's throat. "You don't like me anymore."

"No, I just don't *know* you," Matt corrected. "We went separate ways. Different colleges, different careers."

"But what about Christmas?" Jenna persisted. "Didn't you want to see me then?"

Matt sighed. "I think I saw you through a frosted window once . . . I don't know, five, six years ago."

"Six years?" Jenna shook her head, trying to make sense of it all. "Wasn't I home last Christmas?"

"I don't know, Jenna," Matt said, sounding a little exasperated. "Doesn't your crowd do Saint Barts?" He looked up at the tall apartment building in front of them. "This it?"

Jenna followed his gaze. "Yeah. It's where I live now." Seeing the building again made her stomach flip-flop. She didn't know if she could face going back inside. *I'm only thirteen!* she thought sadly as she clutched her apartment keys.

"Well, okay, it was nice to see you Jenna," Matt said awkwardly. "Good luck."

"Okay," Jenna said, not moving. She was certain she was going to start crying any moment.

"Okay. Goodbye."

"Bye."

Matt gave her a nod, then headed off down the street.

"Matt?" Jenna called out.

"Yeah?"

"Who is Saint Bart?"

Matt stood there and looked at her for a moment. Then, to her relief, he came walking back. "I guess you really do need help."

● ● ●

After Jenna had given Matt a tour of her apartment, he went over to her bookcase to look for her high school yearbook.

"It's got to be here somewhere," he said, rummaging around.

"Maybe I don't have it," Jenna suggested.

Matt snorted. "Oh, you have it. There's no way *you* don't have it . . . aha!" He pulled a large yearbook from the shelf. He scowled at it. "Most dismal years of my life, leather-bound for all posterity."

Jenna sat down at the kitchen table and began thumbing through the yearbook's pages. It was amazing! There were pictures of all the kids she knew from school, but they were four years older! And there were pictures of her, doing things she didn't even remember doing.

She stared at a photo of the Six Chicks, all wearing matching T-shirts.

Jenna was one of them.

"Wow, this is totally weird. I was a Six Chick?"

Matt was looking in the fridge. "You were their leader. Mind if I have a soda?"

Their leader? Me? "Oh, me too! I want one, too."

Matt deposited two soda cans on the table and sat down.

Jenna pointed to one of the girls. "That's Tom-Tom! Oh my God, I wonder what happened to her."

Matt opened his soda. "Well, why don't you ask her?"

Huh? What was he talking about?

"She's your best friend, Jenna," Matt said, as if this was something she already knew. "I think you *work* with her."

The wheels in Jenna's frazzled brain spun for a moment. "Lucy! Oh my God, yes!" That was why she seemed so familiar! "She's Lucy Wyman now. Did she get married?"

"Divorced. Twice."

"She looks so different now," Jenna marveled, remembering the thirteen-year-old Tom-Tom.

"Nose job. Among other things."

Jenna continued to flip through the yearbook. "Ah! I was prom queen?" This was too much. She hadn't just been part of the popular crowd—she'd *ruled* the popular crowd!

"Yup."

"Look, look, look!" Jenna squealed, clutching the yearbook. "I'm so hot! And I went with Chris Grandy?"

"Mmm. Lucky you."

Jenna sat back in her chair. "Wow, Matt. I can't believe it. This is so incredible. I got everything I ever wanted!" She flipped to the next page. "Oh, my God! Wow . . . I'm on every page!" She was practically bouncing in her seat as she went through the yearbook, gazing at images of herself in really cool clothes, hanging out with the most popular kids in school, part of the hottest crowd.

Matt said something just then, and she looked up. He was standing by her window, staring out at the view. "Did you say something?" she asked.

He just looked at her. The phone rang, and Jenna eyed the phone and then Matt.

"It's your phone," he said, as if she had asked him a question.

"Hello?" she said, picking it up.

"Hi, Gramercy calling to confirm your limousine pickup for eight-thirty this evening?"

She let out a squeal. "My limo!" Then she lowered her voice and tried to sound like a grown-up. "Yes, my limousine at eight-thirty this evening. I will be prepared for my ride at that time. Um, could you tell me where I'm going?"

When she got an answer, she scribbled it down on a piece of paper, hung up, and spun around to face Matt. "I'm going to a party! In a limo! Woo-hoo!" She did a little celebratory dance.

"Looks like you're back to normal, Jenna," Matt said, barely cracking a smile. "I should go."

Go? "You don't want to go to the party?" Jenna asked, disappointed.

"I have work to do," Matt said.

"Oh, shoot, I forgot you have a job," Jenna said, wrinkling her nose. "Isn't it cool we both have jobs?"

"Totally," Matt said. But Jenna could tell he wasn't as excited about it as she was. Probably because he had been doing it for a lot longer.

She walked him over to the door. "If you change your mind, you should come. Please, please—it would be so fun! It's at this place." She stared down at a piece of paper in her hand. "Twenty-seven Wall Street."

Matt went to open the door. "Great. Take care, Jenna."

"Matt?" A ripple of fear passed over her.

"What if what I wished for actually happened and I *can't* remember?"

"Hey, you got everything you ever wanted—might as well enjoy it."

Jenna relaxed into a smile. He was right. "Matt?" she said as he opened the door.

"Jenna?"

"Arrivederci."

Finally, something that made Matt smile. Jenna walked toward him.

"Bye, Jenna," Matt said.

"Matt?"

"Yeah?"

Her face was almost touching his. *"Au revoir."*

Matt smiled. "Goodbye."

● ● ●

The rest of the afternoon was the best day of Jenna's life.

First, she took a shower in her fancy marble-tiled bathroom, wrapping herself up in the softest, plushest towels she'd ever used. Then she sat down at her vanity. Boy, did she have a ton of makeup! She tried everything—expensive blush, mascara, pots of lip gloss, fake eyelashes, and lots and lots of glimmery eye shadow. And there were perfume bottles in every shape and size.

Her closet was bigger than her old bedroom. Fancy dresses, soft sweaters in every color of the rainbow, hats, pants, skirts, pocketbooks—and shoes! Not even Nordstrom had this many shoes! She slid her foot into a strappy high heel and let out a squeal.

When Jenna finally left the apartment, she felt like a million bucks. Her hair was piled in a messy updo, and her baby-doll dress swirled with colors. She looked . . . *fabuloso*! When she got on the elevator, there was a thirteen-year-old girl already inside. Jenna gave her a smile. It felt so good to see someone her own age!

"Like your shoes," Jenna told her shyly.

"Thanks," the girl said. She hesitated. "Like your dress." The girl pushed the button to close the doors.

Jenna grinned. "That's because I got these incredible boobs to fill it out!"

The girl gave her a strange look, then stared down forlornly at her own flat chest, hidden under a navy blue polo shirt.

"No! Don't worry!" Jenna hurried to say.

"You've got all *kinds* of time. I didn't grow boobs until—hey! How old are you, anyway?"

"Thirteen," the girl said.

"Me too! Um, used to be. I'm Jenna."

"Yeah, I know," the girl said. "I'm Becky." She seemed surprised that Jenna was even talking to her. Then she confirmed it. "Why are you talking to me?"

"Why not?" Jenna said with a shrug. "We're neighbors, right?"

As they walked out of the elevator, Becky looked at Jenna's purse. "Hey, I really like your bag."

"You should come by sometime," Jenna told her, eager to have a friend. "I've got, like, a zillion."

Becky looked shocked. "Really?"

"Totally!" Jenna said. "It'll be great." Then she lowered her voice. "Um, Becky, can I ask you something? Can you tell that I'm wearing underwear? Because I totally am!" Unless she'd missed something, her grown-up self only wore thongs.

"I think that's kind of the point," Becky said with a giggle.

● ● ● five

"Whoooieeee!" Jenna shrieked, sticking her head and shoulders out of the limousine's sunroof. The early-summer evening air blew her hair, taxi-cabs were honking, the sidewalks were crowded with tourists, and the lights of Times Square were just twinkling on. If only Matt had been here to join her, it would have been perfect!

The *Poise* party was at a really swanky nightspot. There were lots of lights, loud music, and waitresses carrying around trays of yummy-smelling food. Jenna helped herself to a shrimp from a passing tray. She gobbled it up and then, not sure what to do with it, tossed the tail over her shoulder.

"Jenna!" A woman in a fancy dress came walking over with a muscular man. "Hey! You remember my husband, Pete. He's running security again."

Jenna licked cocktail sauce from her fingers. "Oh, great. Hi again," she said, even though she had no idea who either of them were.

"You look lovely this evening," Pete said, taking her hand. He was big and beefy and his meaty hand felt weird holding hers.

"Thanks!" Jenna said, taking her hand back. "Excuse me."

She walked through the crowd, finally spotting Lucy. "Hi, Tom-Tom," she said coyly, coming up behind her.

"Oh God, no one's called me that since my nose job," Lucy said, turning around.

"You got a nose job?" Jenna asked. *Matt was right!*

"Yeah, yeah, it's not as good as yours."

I got a nose job? Jenna reached up to touch her nose.

"Anything to drink, ladies?" asked a passing waitress.

"Apple martini," Lucy said.

"Um . . . lemonade?" Jenna asked. Lucy raised a plucked eyebrow. *Oops, wrong answer!* "No, wait—I'll have a piña colada. *Not* virgin. Do you wanna see my ID? I totally have it."

The waitress shook her head. "That's okay."

"There you two are!" It was Richard. He took Lucy by the arm and checked out her slinky gray and black dress. "Mmm, Lucy, very nice. Kind of a dangerous mermaid look." Then he faced Jenna and his eyes lit up. "And you! Barbie meets Britney! You're just scrum-dilly-icious!"

Jenna beamed at the compliment. "I know! I mean, thanks! Everybody Wang Chung tonight!" As Richard and Lucy stared, she spun around and giggled. Like Matt said, she might as well enjoy it!

● ● ●

There weren't many people dancing on the dance floor. There was a strange, thumping song playing, and instead of singing, someone was yelling over the music. Jenna checked her watch as she walked through the club's upper level, unable to keep a huge grin off her face. She joined Lucy and they walked downstairs. "Eleven o'clock on a school night and I'm at a party! This is so great!"

Lucy looked at Jenna as if she'd lost her mind. "Eleven o'clock and people are *leaving*. This is a disaster."

Jenna frowned. "It is?"

"Speaking of disasters . . . what is she doing here?"

"Who?" Jenna asked.

Lucy's eyes traveled over the crowd to a thin, smug-looking woman with frizzed-out hair. "*Sparkle*'s editor in chief, Trish Sackett, heading our way."

"Hello, girls!" Trish said, sauntering over to them. "Our J.Lo issue is selling like hotcakes. How's *yours* doing?"

"Oh my God, Trish. Are things so bad you had to come to our party for some free food?" Lucy spat out. "Please, throw some crab in your purse for later."

Trish smirked. "Might want to save some

of that cutting wit for your magazine. Or maybe just change your name to something more appropriate, like *Poison* . . . or *Pitiful*. Whatever's more pathetic." Trish winked at Jenna.

A cold, hard rage was filling Jenna's heart. How dare Trish say such mean things? "You are rude and mean, and sloppy and frizzy! I don't like you at *all*!"

Trish looked shocked. "Fortunately, I don't care about being liked. I care about *winning*." With that, she spun on her heel and headed for the exit.

Lucy giggled and gave Jenna a high five.

"Ladies," Richard said, walking over to them. He gestured to his dark gray suit. "Do I *smell*? Do I have bad *breath*? Am I malodorous in any way?"

Lucy rolled her eyes while Jenna shook her head. "No!"

"Because people are running for the exit like someone set off a giant stink bomb."

Jenna began to sniff the air. "I don't smell anything!"

Lucy sighed. "I think he means our party's a stinker. A dud? A flop? Less than zero on a scale of one to ten?"

The sound of another horrible song gave

Jenna an idea. "Um, maybe if we played music that has a melody? I mean, are there still songs that have melodies? Or don't people sing anymore?"

"Honey, play whatever you want to," Richard said, throwing up his hands and gazing over at the bored-looking people gathered near the bar. "All I know is that if we don't get those people dancing and those cameras flashing really, really soon"—he held up his glass as if toasting—"here's to an early retirement! Yippee!" He drank the rest of his drink in one gulp.

Jenna threw back her shoulders and walked over to the DJ's booth. Getting people on the dance floor was one challenge she could easily meet.

The DJ bobbed his head after her request, and seconds later, the opening strains of *Thriller* began to play. Taking a deep breath, Jenna walked out to the desolate dance floor and began to shuffle her feet.

Okay, I feel kind of stupid now, she thought, moving slowly to the center of the dance floor. She gulped as a spotlight was suddenly turned on her. *Shoot!* But there was no way she could stop now. She closed her eyes and tried to get into the music.

After a few minutes, she opened her eyes and there—there was a guy in jeans and a blue shirt—Matt! She waved at him frantically to catch his eye, then motioning to him to come and dance with her. "Matty!" she called, waving some more. "It's *Thriller*!" At last, something people could dance to.

To her dismay, he shook his head. But then the spotlight that had been shining on Jenna swiveled to shine on Matt. A few people began to egg him on.

Jenna ran off the dance floor and grabbed Matt's arm. "You have to help me!" she cried, pulling him. "Come on! You remember the moves!"

"No, actually I don't!" Matt said through gritted teeth.

It didn't matter if he did or didn't. There was no way Jenna was going to continue without him. She dragged him onto the floor and began to dance. She'd practiced the monster dance steps so many times in her room—but this was the first time she was doing them in front of a crowd.

Jenna and Matt locked eyes. Jenna gave him a huge smile and he smiled back. Soon Jenna realized that their dance steps were in sync. Even better, people were beginning to join them on the dance floor.

'Cause this is Thriller, Jenna sang the words in her mind, her arms and legs hitting every synchronized beat. She felt like she was on fire! *This is way better than dancing by myself in front of my mirror*, she thought, beaming as she bobbed her head back and forth to the beat.

She was right in the middle of a spin when Matt took her arm. "I'm sorry, Jenna. I have to go."

"What?" Jenna cried. This was the most fun she'd had since she'd been a grown-up! "No!"

"I shouldn't have come," Matt said. "I'm really sorry. Enjoy your party."

Jenna watched as Matt made his way across the now crowded dance floor. "Matt?" she said, even though she knew he couldn't hear her.

Suddenly, someone grabbed her arm and spun her around. Camera flashes went off. People were smiling and having fun. "I adore you!" Richard said, pulling her into the dancing mob. He kissed her cheek.

Jenna couldn't help it—she laughed and looked around at the happy, bopping crowd. *I did it! I saved the day!*

● ● ●

Dear Diary,

Things just get better every minute! Today I went shopping at Gucci—yes, the real Gucci! And I bought a lot of things that I would never, ever be allowed to wear at home. I eat strawberry ice cream whenever I want to, and I'm not afraid (at least not too much) to make decisions at Poise *anymore. After all, if people think I'm in charge, I better act like I am! Plus, I'm reading this book that explains all sorts of things about magazine publishing. That way I won't look stupid in front of everyone—especially Richard and Lucy.*

Well, that's all for now—I am going to watch a steamy soap show and eat Yodels—IN MY BED!

Here's to being almost thirty!

J

● ● ●

Becka's Bar and Grill was a pretty cool restaurant. The staff of *Poise* ate there a lot. Tonight, Jenna was there with Lucy, and she was on top of the world. She couldn't stop talking about how lucky she was. "I have my own apartment, I can go to bed whenever I want, I've got a Visa card, really cool underwear, and a great bod!" she marveled. "Being a grown-up is awesome!"

Lucy took a small bite of salad. "Of course it is. You're thin, you're hot, and you can get any guy you want, bee-otch!"

Jenna nodded, taking a second to admire her low-cut black dress and matching leather coat. "Not to mention, bee-otch, I'm the hottest magazine editor in the whole world—"

"Second hottest," Lucy corrected.

Jenna's eyes sparkled. "Tied for first?" They exchanged smiles and clinked their glasses.

"Speaking of hot," Lucy said under her breath, putting down her appletini. She leaned closer. "Mr. Hottie at the end of the bar is totally scamming on you right now."

Jenna glanced over her shoulder. *Ooh!* He was cute. "He is not."

"He is," Lucy insisted.

"Should I go talk to him?" Jenna asked nervously. "He's totally cute."

Lucy gave her a coy smile. "You're not married. . . ."

Steeling herself, Jenna got up, gave her short black skirt a tug, and walked past the bar, where all the old guys were, to a table behind them. He was even cuter up close. He was eating a burger and French fries. Jenna guessed he was fourteen.

"So, um, I was wondering if maybe I could borrow your ketchup?" she asked, tucking a strand of hair behind her ear.

"Okay," he said, gaping up at her.

"I just came over here because I think you're really cute," Jenna admitted.

"Do you want to go out sometime?" he asked.

"Okay," Jenna said. "Do you drive?"

Just then Lucy came striding over. She gave the boy a tight-lipped smile and quickly ushered Jenna out of the restaurant. "Do you want to go to *jail?*" Lucy growled. She tilted her head toward a fortysomething guy in a suit at the bar. "I meant *that* guy!"

"Eww, gross!" Jenna said, wrinkling her nose in disgust.

Lucy yanked her outside. "No more daiquiris for you tonight." She pulled out a pack of cigarettes and lit up.

Something across the street caught Jenna's

eye. "Oh my God, it's the naked guy!" She gasped. It was the man from her apartment— the one who was looking for conditioner! He was trying to cross the street to join them, but there was too much traffic.

Lucy flicked her lighter shut. "Where's this alleged hunky teammate he keeps promising to bring me?"

"Hey, beautiful!" he called, waving at Jenna.

"He thinks I'm beautiful?" Jenna said, astonished.

Lucy blew a puff of smoke. "Well, he'd better. He is your boyfriend."

"Boyfriend!" Jenna watched as a woman came running over to him, holding out a piece of paper. She said something to him, and he signed the paper. "Why is that girl asking him for his autograph?"

"Hey, Alex might not be the best New York Ranger, but he is the New York Ranger with the best a—"

"Jenna?" a voice interrupted.

Matt came walking out of Becka's.

"Oh my God, Matt! Hi!"

Lucy squinted at him. "*Beaver*? Is that you?"

"Hello, Tom-Tom. How are you?" Matt asked, sticking his hands in his pockets.

"You lost your baby fat!" Lucy marveled, checking him out. "How does the Beav survive winter?"

"Yeah, it's good to see you, too." Matt peered closely at Lucy's face. "Did you have your nose done again?"

Jenna decided it was time for her to cut in. "What are you doing here?" she asked, thrilled to see Matt. "This is so great!"

Matt glanced back over his shoulder. Jenna followed his gaze and saw a pretty woman walking out of the restaurant.

"I was just having dinner with—" Matt broke off as the woman, smiling, came over and took his hand. "Jenna, Lucy, I'd like you to meet Wendy, my fiancée."

Matt was getting married? Jenna couldn't believe it! As Lucy smiled, Jenna extended her hand. "Oh . . . hi. I'm Jenna."

Wendy snuggled against Matt and shook Jenna's hand with her free one. "So nice to meet you. Matt told me all about his blast from the past. It was really sweet of you to stop by."

"Matty's the sweet one!" Jenna said, wide-eyed. "I don't know what I would have done without him."

Wendy nestled into Matt's arms. "Oh, I'm sure you'll be just fine."

"Are you a photographer, too?" Jenna asked.

A tiny frown flickered across Wendy's face, quickly replaced with a smile. "I see you two spent so much time talking about me!" She cleared her throat. "I do the weather on WWEN in Chicago? Matt and I were just talking about him finally joining me in the Windy City."

Jenna let out a gasp and stared at Matt. "You're moving to Chicago?"

"Yes," Wendy declared.

"We're discussing it," Matt said at the same time. As Wendy gave him a pointed stare, Matt shrugged. "We're figuring it all out."

Suddenly an arm wrapped itself around Jenna's shoulders. Naked guy! Jenna blinked. He was very big, and handsome for an older person. There was something kind of sweet about him, she decided as he kissed the side of her head.

"Hi, Sweetbottom—I mean, Jenna." He

turned to Lucy. "Sorry, Sergei got hit in the mouth with the puck tonight. He sends his regrets."

Lucy rolled her eyes. "He should have sent his replacement."

Jenna was happy to see her so-called boyfriend smile at Matt and Wendy. She hated for anyone to feel left out. "Hi!" Alex said in a friendly voice. "Who are you folks?"

Jenna smiled. "Oh, this is my good friend Matt, and his friend—"

"Fiancée," Wendy corrected. "Wendy."

"Oh, right!" Jenna said, giggling. "That's so weird!" She turned and looked at her boyfriend. How could she introduce him? *I don't even know what his name is!* "This is, um—"

"Alex Carlson," Matt said, grabbing his hand. "Great to meet you. I'm a big fan."

"Thanks," Alex said. "You want me to sign your shirt or forehead or something?" He nudged Matt. "I don't do butts." Alex cracked himself up. "Just joshing. Sorry, I crack a lot of jokes after we win on account of because I get in such a good mood"—he turned to Jenna—"which I'll prove to you later!"

Now Alex gave Jenna a nudge. She forced

out a tiny laugh. Whatever he meant by that, it didn't sound good.

"Well, we better run," Matt said as Wendy tugged on his hand. "Great to meet you."

"Nice to see you," Alex called out after them. "Bye!"

Jenna watched Matt and Wendy walk down the city street. It was so weird to think of Matt with a girlfriend—not to mention a fiancée!

"Lucy, you mind if I steal her from you for the rest of the night?" Alex said, startling Jenna.

"Steal away," Lucy said, gazing back at someone inside the restaurant. "I've got my eyes on something better inside."

"Um, excuse me one sec?" Jenna said to Alex. She pulled Lucy aside. "Should I go over to his place? *Alone?*" The idea seemed pretty scary. Jenna knew she looked like a grown-up, but she definitely *wasn't* one—and she definitely didn't want to get into any kind of weird grown-up situation. "Why not?" Lucy said. "Go play. You've earned it."

"Play?" Jenna repeated, a bit confused. "Like games and stuff?"

Lucy gave her a wink. "Yes, all *kinds* of games."

Alex's apartment was really cool. He had a huge TV hanging on the wall, unlike any TV Jenna had ever seen. It was completely flat! There were lots of pictures of Alex in his hockey uniform, skating across the ice with a hockey stick. And he had a killer stereo system that was playing some sort of jazz music.

Jenna sat fidgeting on a leather couch. *I'm in a boy's apartment! Wait a minute, no, I'm in a* man's *apartment. Even worse!*

"I couldn't wait to see you tonight," Alex murmured, sitting down beside her.

"Okay, turn around!" Jenna burst out. "I wanna do something to you."

"You do, do ya?" Alex said, laughing. "Hmmm, what do you have up your sleeve, my little vixen?"

Alex did as she'd asked and Jenna got up on her knees on the couch. She put her finger on his back. "Going on a treasure hunt, X marks the spot! Dot-dash-dot-dash, big question mark!" She moved her finger along with her words. "Spiders crawling up your back, blood gushing down." She blew on his neck. "Cool breeze, tight squeeze!" She grabbed him. "Gotcha!"

"You are so hammered," Alex said, turning back around. "C'mere, you."

He pulled her close and Jenna realized he was going to kiss her. Her stomach was a sea of nerves. She giggled.

"What?" Alex said, pulling back.

"Nothing."

But as soon as he moved closer, the giggles started up again.

"Hey, if you don't want to—" Alex began.

"Sorry," Jenna said between giggles. "I'm sorry. Let's just . . . play a game! Do you have Battleship?"

Alex stood up and, to Jenna's shock, began to dance. Then he started unbuttoning his shirt.

"What are you doing?" Jenna shrieked as Alex moved his shoulders up and down.

"I owe you one raunchy striptease, if I'm not mistaken."

Jenna frowned and scooted back. "What if we watch TV instead?"

But Alex wasn't stopping. Instead, he began unzipping his pants. "What if we go on a treasure hunt instead?"

Jenna recoiled in horror as Alex's pants dropped to the floor. He stood there in his underpants! He had a goofy smile on his lips, and he kept swiveling his hips to the music.

"Who's got the moves off the ice, ice, baby?" he cooed.

"Gross!" Jenna yelped, covering her eyes. In a desperate attempt to get away, she backed up and fell onto the couch, bounced off, and landed on the floor.

"Gross?" Alex repeated, stopping his dance.

Jenna hid behind a sofa pillow. She took a peek at him. "Ugh!" she shouted, waving her hands at him. "Aughhh! I don't want to see *that* again! Don't you have any board games, like Monopoly or Yahtzee?"

● ● ● six

The next morning, Jenna, wearing a designer suit, her hair held up in a bun by chopsticks, got on the elevator with Becky. She recognized the look on her friend's face: misery. "You wanna talk about it?" Jenna asked.

Becky hesitated. "All the cool girls are having a sleepover Friday night. And I'm not invited."

Jenna could empathize. "That sucks."

"Totally," Becky agreed dolefully.

Jenna thought of how the Six Chicks had

treated her . . . and how things had ended up. "Listen. Those girls don't know anything about being cool."

● ● ☻

As Jenna approached the front door of *Poise,* she ate a jelly donut. A little glob of jelly squirted out on her chin. As she wiped it off, an annoying high-pitched voice reached her ears. "If it isn't the little drama queen."

Jenna turned. It was Trish Sackett. Jenna's eyes narrowed. This was one mean, mean grown-up.

"That was a bit much the other night, don't you think?" Trish asked.

"I think your attitude was a bit much!" Jenna said, indignant.

Trish sighed. "All right, fine, let's give it a rest." Then she brightened. "Did you hear? Our circulation is at nine hundred thousand. Cancel all plans for a long career at *Poise.*"

"'Cancel all plans for a long career at *Poise,*'" Jenna mimicked.

"Hey!" Trish said peevishly. "What bug got up your butt?"

"*You* are the big ugly bug that I wouldn't let *near* my butt!" And with that, Jenna stormed through the front entrance of *Poise*.

● ● ●

Lots of mornings at *Poise* were spent in meetings. This one was no different. Jenna sat in the conference room with a bunch of other people who worked there. They all drank lots and lots of coffee, while she usually had something yummy, like a fruit roll-up. On today's agenda was trying to come up with some catchy lines to put on the cover of the magazine. But no one had any good ideas. Some of them were so dumb, Jenna couldn't help laughing.

She quieted down when Richard walked into the room. He didn't look happy. "There's no easy way to say this, so I'll just come out with it," he said, clearing his throat. "The circs are in. Our numbers are dismal. We're below six hundred thousand in total circulation. *Sparkle* is closing in on a million."

Everyone gasped, even Jenna.

"I just got off the phone with corporate. They dropped the *R* word."

More gasps. This time, Jenna was lost.

"Redesign?" a staffer named Tracy asked, dismayed. "Redesign *Poise*?"

"Wait, wait, wait," Glenn interjected. *Sparkle* copies everything we come up with, everything we do, and *we* have to redesign? That's total bull!"

Everyone nodded and voiced his or her opinion.

"We haven't been given a choice," Richard declared, raising his hands. "We've been given an ultimatum. Either we redesign and bring up our numbers . . . or they pull the plug."

Now the room was totally quiet.

Lucy groaned. "Richard, redesign is a death sentence."

"No!" Jenna burst out. "No, it's a chance to have some fun! Let *Sparkle* have all our stale, secondhand, grody ideas. We'll open up our F.O.B., overhaul the B.O.B.—so let's all of us pull together and prove that we've got some poise *left*."

● ● ●

When Jenna headed back toward her office, Arlene was waiting for her in the corridor. She held a stack of message slips.

Jenna and Matt admire the Dream House.

Jenna is now a grown-up and her wish has come true!

Jenna loves her amazing wardrobe
and walk-in closet.

Jenna enjoys a ride through Times Square.

Jenna and Lucy worry that the *Poise* party is a flop.

Jenna leads the crowd with her dance moves.

Alex surprises Jenna with some moves of his own.

Jenna is hard at work at *Poise*.

Jenna asks Matt to do the photo shoot.

Jenna and Matt's Class of 2004.

Jenna and Matt look over the photos.

Jenna and Matt take a lovely walk.

Jenna enjoys a slumber party with the girls.

Jenna reveals a whole new look for *Poise*.

Jenna presents her redesign.

Jenna looks forward to celebrating with Matt.

"Well, that was a bummer," Jenna said, trying not to let Richard's news get her down.

"I have your urgent messages," Arlene said, walking alongside her.

"Oh, I have such an achy head," Jenna moaned. Ever since she became a grown-up, people always had things to tell her! "Would you just read 'em to me real quick? Pretty please."

"Um, well, okay," Arlene said, clearing her throat. "Emily Pratt called and wanted me to tell you, 'I can't believe you scooped my story on Vivienne Tam, you backbiting little bitch. That was a new level of sleaze even for you. I hope you die in one of her casual fall pantsuits.'"

"That's so mean!" Jenna exclaimed. She took the messages from Arlene's hand. "Why don't I just look at them later?"

Arlene seemed relieved. "Good. Great."

Dejected, Jenna sat down at her desk. She picked up a fuzzy pen and twirled it between her fingers.

Arlene's voice came over the intercom on Jenna's desk. "Alex is on line one?"

"Yuck," Jenna mumbled. She pushed the response button. "Could you please tell Alex I'm busy?"

"He wants to know what time is good for dinner."

"How about in ten zillion years?" Jenna said, wanting to stay as far away from him and his awful dancing as possible. "Is that good?"

Arlene giggled. "I don't know, I'll ask." The intercom beeped off.

Jenna picked up a Hello Kitty notebook and started jotting down some ideas. The intercom buzzed again. "I'm sorry to bother you again," Arlene said. "Pete Hansen is here to see you?"

"Who?" Jenna asked.

"Tracy from the art department's husband?"

"Oh, okay, sure," Jenna said, remembering them from the party. She stood up as Arlene walked him in.

"I was just dropping off Tracy's lunch, and I thought I'd say hello," Pete explained.

"You bring Tracy her lunch?" Jenna said, touched. Arlene left, closing the door behind her. "That is sooo sweet of—"

Suddenly Pete grabbed her and began trying to kiss her. Grossed out completely, Jenna pushed him away. "What are you doing?" she shrieked.

"What's wrong, Pooky?" Pete said, moving in to kiss her again.

"Um, Pukey, you're married?" Jenna said sarcastically, trying to dodge his greasy grasp. "To someone I work with?"

Pete smirked. "That didn't stop us from rattling some desk drawers last week. So come on—lie down and take a memo." He lifted her up toward the desk and Jenna kneed him in the groin. With an *"Oof!"* he fell to the floor.

"When you can walk again," Jenna said breathlessly, "please walk really fast, out this door." And then, before he could pull any other moves, she walked out herself.

Jenna's heart was beating so fast she thought it would burst out of her chest. That had been the grossest experience of her life! She gulped some air and tried to steady herself as she passed the door of the art department. Whispers were coming from inside. Jenna stopped to listen.

"I don't want Jenna involved *at all*. If corporate goes with our plan, we're sitting very pretty. Hire the best photographer you can find and let's *move* on this."

Jenna's mouth fell open. It was Lucy.

"Roger that," came a voice that Jenna recognized as belonging to Lucy's assistant, Rachel. "What is up with Jenna, anyway? She seems . . . lost."

"She is," Lucy said. "She's lost her edge, she's dull—love her to death, but my God, isn't her Suzy Cheerleader routine just hysterical?"

"Let's all pull together and show we still have poise," Rachel said in a voice Jenna realized was supposed to be her own. "Gag me."

Jenna wrapped her arms around herself as the two women she thought were her friends began to laugh.

She had never felt so alone.

● ● ●

Back in her apartment that night, Jenna gazed out her windows, looking at the city lights twinkling and the traffic swirling by. A sad song played on her stereo. She twirled her ponytail around her finger, staring off into space. She felt small. *I've got this amazing apartment, a cool job, and this killer body . . . but what I really need is a friend.*

There was only one place she could think of to go.

Fifteen minutes later, she was pounding on Matt's apartment door.

"Okay, you're not Cajun," he said, opening the door. His hair was all rumpled and he was wearing faded jeans and no socks.

Jenna bit her lip. Wasn't she better than a food delivery person? "Do you want to do something? Hang out?"

Matt blinked. "You mean now?"

Jenna nodded.

He studied her. "What's wrong?"

"I—I'm lonely," Jenna admitted.

"And you came all the way down here?" Matt shook his head. "Jenna, why didn't you just call someone?"

"'Cause you're the person I wanted to see."

After Matt grabbed his wallet and turned off his lights, the two of them went outside and began walking uptown. "I still can't believe you're getting married," Jenna said, kicking a pebble.

"In two weeks."

Jenna looked at her friend. He didn't sound very happy about it. "Is she, like, your soul mate?"

"My soul mate." He paused. "You know, I don't think I believe in those. I think that's kind of naïve."

"But when you see her now, she gives you goose bumps, right?" Jenna was eager to know. "Do you get butterflies in your stomach?"

Matt smiled. "I haven't gotten all crazy like that since I was a kid, thank goodness."

Jenna came to a stop. The Matt she knew, the Matt who was her friend—was this really how he ended up? Why? What went wrong? She looked down at the ground. "Matt? What happened to us? How come we never stayed friends?"

Matt stopped walking, too. "I—I don't know."

That wasn't good enough. "Matty, what happened?"

"Well . . . I think I can pretty much peg it to your thirteenth-birthday party."

She could feel the blood surging through her veins. *The party . . .*

"You were playing that game in the closet. What's it called?"

"Seven Minutes in Heaven," Jenna

answered. "Everybody ditched me. It's the last thing I remember."

Now Matt looked uncomfortable. "Look, Jenna, we really don't need to get into this. It doesn't matter anymore."

"It does to me," Jenna insisted. "Please, Matt."

He sighed. "Okay. When you came out of the closet I started playing my electric guitar and singing my Jenna song, and you threw at me, with impressive force, I might add, that silly dream house I spent three weeks building."

Tears filled her eyes. How could she have been so mean?

"And after that, you cut me off," Matt said quietly. "Wouldn't talk to me. Ever."

"Matt—" The words caught in Jenna's throat. "I'm so sorry."

"Forget it," Matt said, shaking his head. "It's a long time ago."

Jenna stomped her foot. "Would you please stop being so nice to me? Do you know what kind of person I am now? Right now?" She waved her hands in the air. "I don't have any friends, I think I did something really, really gross with a married guy, I don't even talk to my mom and dad—I'm not a nice person. And guess what?" Jenna knew her face was blotchy and her nose was running, but it didn't matter. "I'm not thirteen anymore." She turned and began walking away.

"Jenna!" Matt called after her.

She picked up her pace. There was somewhere she had to go to right away.

• ● ●

The spare house key was right where it always had been, inside the flowerpot on the front stoop. Jenna unlocked the door and stepped inside her house. It was quiet.

She walked upstairs and pushed open her bedroom door. Her posters, stuffed animals, plastic leis, photographs in neon-colored frames—everything was gone. *They turned my room into a gym.* She saw a treadmill, a set of free weights, and some weird contraption for reducing your waistline that she had seen on a late-night infomercial.

Lost in thought, Jenna walked over to her dresser, picked up her Cabbage Patch Kid, and held it close. The doll still had its familiar smell. This doll was the only proof she had even existed in this house. It was all that was left of her childhood. *Except maybe . . .*

Jenna went downstairs and headed for the basement. It looked pretty much the same as she remembered. She walked to the closet, turned on the light, and sat down inside. Above her, toys and old board games crowded the shelves. Jenna began rocking back and forth. *What have I done to my life?* she thought sadly as a tear slid down her cheek. How had it all gone so wrong?

Her old Battleship game fell from the shelf onto her head. Jenna didn't flinch. Instead, she continued rocking.

Suddenly the closet door flew open. Her parents stood there, her father wielding a golf umbrella. Her father's hair had turned slightly gray, and her mom had a few more laugh lines around her lips and eyes, but other than that, they looked exactly the same.

"Jenna?" her mother gasped.

Her father lowered the umbrella as a jigsaw puzzle crashed to the floor, scattering its pieces. "Honey, what on earth?"

Jenna leapt to her feet and threw her arms around her parents. "I missed you so much!"

Her mother hugged her, then pulled back. "You okay, sweetie?"

"Can I stay with you guys tonight?" Jenna asked, overwhelmed with happiness. *Who would have ever dreamt I'd be so happy to see my parents?* she thought as they exchanged surprised yet happy smiles.

Being home in her regular old New Jersey house on Spruce Street with Bev and Wayne Rink was suddenly very, very cool.

● ● ● seven

Jenna sighed with pleasure as she savored a mouthful of chocolate chip pancakes. After weeks of bagels and cold cereal that she'd prepared herself, it felt wonderful to have someone take care of her.

The night before, there had been a terrible thunderstorm. Jenna had crept from the den, where she was sleeping, and had crawled into bed with her parents. For the first time since her life had gone topsy-turvy, she had fallen asleep instantly.

That's why I feel so refreshed this morning, she thought happily as her mom took her plate.

"Mom?" she said. "You ever wish you could go back? I mean, to another time?"

Bev Rink smiled. "I wouldn't mind giving back some of these wrinkles."

"No, really," Jenna said, insistent. "I mean, what would you do over if you could? *Anything,* in your whole life."

Her mom paused for a moment, leaning against the kitchen counter. Then she smiled and shook her head. "Nothing."

"Really?" Jenna said, incredulous.

Her mom nodded.

"But what about really big mistakes?" Jenna asked. Surely her mom would want to take those back. "The huge ones, ones that change your life forever?"

"Jenna, I made a lot of mistakes, sure," her mother said, sitting down at the table and resting her hand on Jenna's knee. "But I don't regret making them."

"But why not?"

"Well, sweetie, because I wouldn't have gotten anywhere without them."

● ● ●

After Jenna had said her goodbyes to her parents and had taken the train back into the city, she'd holed up in her apartment. She'd taken with her boxes full of mementos of her childhood—photographs, cards, yellowed cutouts from eighties magazines. She even found a pink satin headband Matt had given her.

Now she sat on the floor, a steaming mug of hot chocolate at her side, soaking all her memories up. She had collected some great stuff. And there had to be a way to put it to use.

Jenna picked up her old yearbook and began thumbing through it. She smiled as she looked at all the silly, kooky pictures. Then, suddenly, something hit her. She grabbed a pair of scissors and began cutting pages from the yearbook. Photographs that showed kids having a great time—two kids on a tandem bike riding past the high school eating ice cream cones, kids sledding on the hill and having a snowball fight, the senior class posed on the high school's front steps, leaning on each other and laughing . . .

The photographs were warm and beautiful.

Jenna noticed a pair of initials in the corner of one: M.F. Flipping through her pile, she realized that all the photos she had cut out had been taken by M.F. *Matt Flamhaff.*

Jenna smiled and shook her head. *Of course.*

● ● ●

At work the next day, Jenna had Arlene gather a stack of back issues of *Sparkle* and *Poise.* She went through them, circling words like *cool* and *hip* and *in,* then tore out the pages. She also ripped out pages of models who looked sick, malnourished, or depressed. *Yuck!* No wonder these issues bombed. Jenna was so into her work, she didn't even realize that it had turned dark outside her office window.

As Jenna was leaving her floor to go home, she caught a glimpse of Lucy getting on an empty elevator. She reached in and stopped the doors from closing.

"Oh, hey!" Lucy looked surprised to see her. She had a large satchel over her shoulder.

"Hey," Jenna said. It had been days since they had spoken.

"I was going to stop by your office," Lucy said as the elevator slid downward. "I tried calling you a bunch of times."

"I didn't get any messages," Jenna said. She knew it was a lie. Lucy hadn't called her. *I know what you said to Rachel!* she thought, fighting back the urge to call her on it.

Lucy brushed it off. "I was in a hurry. I did try to reach you, though." She cleared her throat. "Listen, Jenna, um . . . I've been meaning to tell you . . . about the redesign thing? I'm actually kind of throwing something together on my own. It's very last-minute." She gave a helpless little shrug. "Hope you don't mind."

"No, of course not," Jenna said, the flutter of competition tingling through her veins.

Lucy smiled and squeezed Jenna's arm as the elevator doors opened.

"Because I'm doing the same thing," Jenna said with a smile of her own. Shaking free of Lucy's grasp, she exited through *Poise*'s revolving glass door into the New York night.

● ● ●

The next morning when Jenna entered the lobby at *Poise*, she found herself stuck in an elevator with Lucy. Neither of them spoke for the entire ride up. When the elevator arrived on their floor, Jenna stepped out and walked past the security desk.

Shoot! There was Alex, pleading with the security guard to let him in.

Jenna tried to scoot by undetected.

"Hey, Jenna!" he called out.

Jenna turned back and gave him a small smile. "Hi, Alex."

He jogged over to her, and Jenna gave the security guard a look that said it was okay. "I was just coming to see you but they wouldn't let me up," Alex told her. "What's the deal? I mean, I got your message. A zillion years? That's like a really long time."

Jenna scrunched up her face in the most sympathetic way she knew how and nodded. She hadn't had much experience breaking up with people—but at the very least, she could do it nicely.

"Whoa, whoa, whoa," Alex said, holding up his hands. "Wait a minute. Are you breaking up with me?"

Jenna nodded once more.

Alex looked stunned. "You're tough.

That's . . . wow. This is deep. Nobody's ever broken up with me." He bent over and put his hands on his knees, as though the wind had been knocked out of him. "This hurts," he managed to get out. "This is powerful stuff."

Jenna bit her lip. "I'm sorry. Are you okay?"

He held up one hand, as if to say *Don't worry, I'll survive.* "No pain, no gain, right?"

Jenna smiled. "That's a nice way to look at it."

"I'm never going to forget you, Sweetbottom," he said, finally standing upright.

"Jenna," she corrected politely.

"Yeah, right," Alex said, looking sheepish. "Jenna." Then his eyes lit up. "You know what I'm going to do? I'm going to score a goal for you. You watch. *Pow!* When you see me go like this on TV"—he pointed his finger like a gun—"that's *your* goal."

"Okay," Jenna said, backing up. "Well, I better get going."

"Oh, right, yeah, you're busy," Alex said, nodding. "I know. Anyway, I feel loads better. Thanks. See ya. *Pow!*"

Jenna couldn't wait for her plans to unfold. She stood at the edge of Central Park, across from the Museum of Natural History, rocking back and forth on her toes. Then she spotted Matt, jogging up from the subway stop.

"Hey," Matt said, walking to her.

"You bring it?" Jenna asked, eyeing his bulging backpack.

He opened it up to reveal several high-tech cameras. "I brought a few. Are you going to tell me what we're doing here?"

Jenna smiled. "No . . . but I'll show you." She began pulling him toward the park. Once inside, they rounded a bend, and Jenna beamed. A photo crew was setting up for an elaborate shoot. Male and female models were using a parked bus as a dressing room. A large table stood covered with platters of bagels, cream cheese, and coffee urns. Camera tripods, electronic equipment, and light reflectors were everywhere.

"Wow, someone's got a big shoot going," Matt said, taking it all in. "Hey!" He pointed to some models wearing cheerleaders' uniforms. "That's just like our high school's uniform!"

He turned to Jenna, who was grinning from ear to ear. "Jenna, what's going on?"

She handed him a check for five thousand dollars.

"What's this?" he asked, confused.

"I'm hiring you," she explained, beaming. "Actually, *Poise* is hiring you. For the week."

"Whoa, whoa, whoa!" Matt exclaimed. "Jenna, thank you. I mean, I could use this—but you don't have to do me any favors here." He tried to hand the check back, but Jenna refused to accept it.

"You're doing *me* the favor," she told him. "I love your work. I want you to do this."

"But, Jenna, I've looked at your magazine," Matt protested. "This isn't your style . . . at all."

Jenna laughed. "Exactly."

● ● ●

The photo shoots that took place over the next week went better than Jenna could ever have imagined. Cheerleaders led cheers in front of bleachers, where fans, decked out in autumn colors, cheered and huddled together. A wind machine blew leaves toward the models as Matt snapped frame after frame.

A crew guy passing by with a ladder bumped into the support pole of the wind machine, sending it toppling. Now huge piles of leaves blew toward the models, Matt, and Jenna. The models ran for cover, but Jenna loved it. She did a little dance in the swirling leaves as Matt took more pictures, this time of her.

A few days later Jenna stood on a Manhattan rooftop that had been transformed into the setting for a fantasy high school prom. A banner read WINTER WONDERLAND. Matt took photo after photo as models danced past in sleek tuxedos and organza dresses, fake snow falling on their shoulders. She clasped her hands together in delight as the models dipped ladles into a punch bowl while a band played on a small stage. She grabbed Matt's hand and dragged him onto the dance floor.

This is even better than a real prom, Jenna decided as she twirled into Matt's arms. And she wasn't sure if it was the fake snow or Matt's smile—but something gave her goose bumps.

The last shoot of the week was on the steps of the New York Public Library. Twenty-four models stood dressed as different city types—Wall Street brokers, a bike messenger, schoolgirls, hip-hop guys, socialites, a chef—as a fake photographer with an old-style camera and flashbulb pretended to take the Class of 2004's picture.

Matt shot a few frames, but Jenna could tell by his expression that he wasn't happy with the result.

It's too stiff and posed, Jenna realized. She signaled to some crew guys who were standing off to the side, holding balloons that were to be used later. "Drop the balloons," she mouthed. And as hundreds of brilliant-colored balloons descended on the group, Matt took the perfect unrehearsed "class photo."

● ● ●

"They're beautiful," Jenna murmured as she and Matt huddled together over a light box at a Brooklyn photo studio, looking at the finished images of the Rooftop Prom.

"Came out okay, huh?" Matt asked, putting down his loupe.

"You think so?" Jenna said.

He smiled. "I do."

She smiled back. "Me too."

"The rest will be ready Wednesday morning around eleven." Matt held up his hands in a helpless gesture. "I'm stuck here in Brooklyn all day shooting a brochure for Centrum. It's actually a good gig—it's like the Swimsuit Edition of the vitamin world."

Jenna snatched the receipt for the film from the table. "Don't worry! I'll pick them up."

Matt grinned. "Lab's on Twenty-third between Fifth and Sixth." Then he just looked at her, as if he was going to add something more. "Well, I should get going, I guess," he said finally. "It's—"

"You know what I'm in the mood for?" Jenna interrupted, not wanting their time together to end. She put on a serious look. "Razzles."

"Razzles?" Matt looked pleased. "Wow! I haven't had Razzles in fifteen years."

"They're both a candy *and* a gum," Jenna reminded him. "I'm treating. You in?"

Matt tucked his arm through hers. "You know what? I think I *need* some Razzles."

● ● ●

After splurging on a huge sackful of Razzles, Jenna and Matt walked along the Promenade in Brooklyn, eating candy together. Matt broke into a smile and shook his head.

"What's so funny?" Jenna asked.

"Life. Timing. Being here with you, eating

Razzles." Matt looked into her eyes. "It's just been a really great week—I mean working with you, and . . . everything."

Jenna smiled. "Me too." They walked a little more, and then she stood still. "Hey, is my tongue blue?" She stuck her tongue way out. "What color is my tongue?" she pressed.

"Red," Matt said.

"Razzle red or tongue red?" Jenna asked.

Matt grinned. "Razzle red."

"Let me see yours," Jenna asked.

"I'm not showing you my tongue!" Matt said, laughing.

Jenna would have none of that. "Let me see your tongue, Matt! Come on! I showed you mine!"

"I didn't *ask* to see it."

Jenna's eyes grew deadly serious. "I need to see your tongue." She gave him a prompting stare. "Matty."

Matt groaned. "Okay, here." He stuck his tongue out.

Jenna rocked back on her heels, pleased. "Razzle red." She leaned over. "You want to know a secret? You're the sweetest guy I've ever known."

Matt was quiet for a moment. Then he

grinned and nodded toward the playground. "And I can still kick your butt off the jump."

Just like old times, they each hopped onto a swing and began pumping their legs to see who could go higher.

"Okay, whoever lands furthest, the other one owes him a drink," Matt declared.

"An Orange Julius!" Jenna called out, naming her favorite orange slushy beverage.

"Ooh, uppin' the stakes," Matt teased, pumping higher.

"And dinner Wednesday night at eight o'clock at the . . . Forty-second Street Diner, to celebrate our redesign being chosen!"

"Deal," Matt said, pumping hard. "Okay, one, two, three!"

Whoosh! Jenna pumped her legs in one last heroic effort, then let go. She and Matt sailed off their swings and hit the ground, rolling and tumbling into each other.

"Are you all right?" Jenna asked between giggles. She felt as if they were one giant human pretzel.

"Good thing I remembered to tuck and roll," Matt said with a groan. "Man, I'm getting old!"

"You are not!" Jenna said firmly. "'Cause that means I am!"

"Well . . ."

Jenna gave him a swat as they started to untangle themselves. Then she stared at his arm. "You've got arm hair," she said, amazed. She brushed it lightly with her fingertips.

"It's never gotten quite this reaction before," Matt murmured, looking at her.

A tingle began in Jenna's toes and crept slowly up her body. *He's going to kiss me!* she realized, filled with a nervous giddiness. For a moment she was sure she had stopped breathing. Matt moved closer. And then Jenna closed her eyes and they were kissing.

Jenna pulled back, breathing hard.

"I, uh, better get going," Matt mumbled, drawing his hand across his lips.

"Right. Okay," Jenna said as her heart continued to thump.

Nothing would ever be the same again.

●　●　●

"It was like it wasn't even me, like I came out of my body. Just me going up and seeing us down below, kissing." Jenna smiled as she recalled her moment with Matt, hugging a pillow to her chest. "And then I floated home . . . on a cloud," she finished.

The five thirteen-year-old girls who sat in a circle on Jenna's bed let out a collective sigh.

"Oh, Jenna," Sara said, munching on some popcorn. "That is sooooo romantic!"

Jenna nodded happily. She had been so excited after her day with Matt that she had to share it with someone. Inviting Becky from her building and her four best friends—Catherine, Gina, Sara, and Sydney—to a sleepover had been the perfect solution.

Jenna pulled up her pajama sleeve to show the girls her arm.

"Oh my God!" Catherine exclaimed, examining Jenna's skin.

"You've got goose bumps!" Gina said.

"I totally know!" Jenna squealed. "They won't go away!"

Sydney rocked back on her heels. "Do you love him?"

Jenna felt her cheeks flush. She giggled and hid behind her hands. Did she? She thought maybe she did!

"When are you going to see him again?" Gina wanted to know.

Jenna slumped down a bit, instantly deflated. "Well, actually . . . I don't think I can."

"What?" the girls cried in unison.

"It's kind of complicated," Jenna admitted. "It's a grown-up thing."

Everyone, including Jenna, was quiet for a moment.

Catherine nibbled some popcorn. "At least you have someone to dream about," she said brightly.

"Yeah," Sydney agreed. "Boys don't actually want to jump your bones when you are wearing headgear." She pointed to her braces.

"Let me tell you something," Jenna said earnestly. "I know it's torture to wear that now, but someday soon you're going to be beautiful. I can see. All of you. The guys are going to be lining up."

But none of the girls believed her. "I don't think so," Sara said.

Becky nodded glumly. "No way."

Catherine, Gina, and Sydney looked similarly bummed.

"Hey!" Jenna exclaimed passionately.

"What kind of attitude is that? We are *young*! Heartache to heartache, we *stand*. No one ever said it would be easy. *Love* is a *battlefield*."

"Wow," the girls murmured, awed.

"That is sooo true," Becky murmured.

"It's a total battlefield," Sarah said, her eyes wide "That's really deep."

"Can you write it down?" Becky asked.

Jenna paused. "I could. Or . . ." She sprang to her feet and put *All Fired Up: The Very Best of Pat Benatar* into the CD player. Moments later, Pat Benatar's immortal words began bursting through the speakers. *"We are young, heartache to heartache, we stand!"*

And then, with spoons, Diet Coke cans, and body lotion bottles for microphones, Jenna and her thirteen-year-old friends rocked out.

• • • eight

Jenna pulled back, surveying her work. She, Arlene, and Tracy were in the art department at *Poise*, where they had just finished laying Matt's photographs on one large posterboard and Jenna's clipped-out magazine words on another.

"What do you think?" Jenna asked, excitement building inside her. The photographs were so great. She crossed her fingers and hoped Arlene and Tracy felt the same way.

"Well, Jenna, I think I'm going to start

reading *Poise*," Arlene said. She looked around to make sure no one was walking by. "For the first time in my life!"

"Me too!" Tracy added excitedly, clasping her hands together.

All three of them let out a shriek.

It's going to work! Jenna thought, squeezing her friends' fingers. *It's got to!*

Just as she had when she'd given a science class presentation on metamorphosis, Jenna worked furiously on her ideas for the redesign, using a Magic Marker to write on construction paper, cutting out more clips from old magazines, and jotting notes in a book.

I wonder if the prints are ready? she thought, hopping up to check with Arlene. When she turned the corner near the art department, she bumped right into Richard. He was in quite a mood.

"Jenna! Lucy's presenting her own redesign without you? What is going on around here?"

Jenna skidded to a halt. "What's going on is, well, you're going to have . . . more choices."

Richard folded his arms across his chest. "Jenna, with all due respect to Lucy, I'm far more anxious to know what *you've* been working on."

Jenna smiled. "Thank you."

"I'm not trying to compliment you," Richard said, sounding fed up. "I'm trying to *pressure* you."

If she hurried . . . "Can you give me till five?" she asked.

Richard ran a hand across his brow. "Jenna, you're not yourself lately. Since when do you keep me out of the loop? I'm freaking out here!"

Arlene waved frantically to Jenna. "Prints are ready!"

"Oh, great!" Jenna turned to Richard. "Hang in there, Richard. Gotta go!" Then she turned to Arlene, who hadn't moved from her desk. "Well, aren't you coming?"

A startled but pleased-looking Arlene got up and scurried after Jenna down the hall.

"Go, go!" Richard shouted after them. "What do I know? I'm *just* the editor in chief."

● ● ●

If Jenna and Arlene had stayed, they would have witnessed one of the worst presentations the staff at *Poise* had ever seen.

The redesign ideas of Lucy Wyman.

With techno music blaring as a backdrop,

Lucy had concocted a flashy PowerPoint demonstration of her ideas. "The new and improved *Poise* will explore the last frontier. It will go heroin chic one better. It will OD. It will kill! Cause of death? Chicness," she said, her voice dramatic. "The new *Poise* will go further than any fashion magazine before. It will be deadly serious. Fashion suicide."

Richard turned off the music and the lights came back on in the *Poise* conference room.

"So, what do you think?" Lucy asked anxiously, scanning the faces of her colleagues.

And after Richard told her, and the other staffers nodded in silent agreement, Lucy stormed out and dumped her portfolio in a trash bin.

As Lucy strode past Jenna's open office door, she noticed that Arlene was gone. Lucy hesitated for a moment and then walked inside. Her eyes fell on Jenna's design boards.

So this is what she's been working on, she thought, seething. *She thinks she's going to top me, does she?*

Then Lucy's eyes fell on a small white envelope that had already been opened. She picked it up. The envelope was addressed to Jenna's residence, and the return address said *Trish Sackett*.

Lucy slid out the contents. "Oh, my," she breathed, dropping into Jenna's chair. It was a copy of *Sparkle*'s most recent cover, the "J.Lo's Eleventh Secret" cover. A handwritten note was paper-clipped to it.

Dear Jenna,
Thanks so much for helping us make this a great cover. The twelfth secret is that you're going to be the best editor in chief in the city, right here at Sparkle*! Shhh!*
Trish

Without hesitating a moment, Lucy picked up Jenna's phone and punched in Trish's number. "Trish Sackett, please," she said, the wheels in her brain spinning with possibility. "Lucy Wyman calling."

● ● ●

"Oh my God!" Jenna shrieked as she and Arlene climbed out of a cab. Jenna's hand flew to her face.

"What? What?" Arlene cried.

"The—the things! The things!" Jenna

shouted, waving her arms around. They had forgotten to pick up the blowups! All this work had made mush of her brain.

"What things?" Arlene asked, bewildered.

"The big blowup things!" Jenna absolutely had to have them for her presentation.

"Oh, those things," Arlene said, nodding fast. "We have time. Let's just go get those things." She led a frazzled Jenna back toward the cab.

Jenna threw herself into the black pleather seat as Arlene rattled off the address. Everything had to be perfect—the future of *Poise* depended on it.

● ● ●

While Jenna was frantically trying to gather everything she needed to make a fabulous presentation, Matt Flamhaff decided to visit her at her office. There was something he needed to tell her. Something that couldn't wait.

"Jenna?" Matt said as he walked down the plush office hallway, locating her nameplate outside her office. She was on the phone, her back turned. He knocked lightly on the door and entered.

The problem was, it wasn't Jenna.

The chair swiveled around. "Hi, Beaver—oops, I mean, Matt." Lucy Wyman smiled coolly up at him. "Sorry. Old habits die so hard. How *are* you?"

"Hey, is Jenna here?" he asked, ignoring the putdown. He gazed around at the empty office, hoping that somehow Jenna would pop out from behind a filing cabinet.

Lucy rolled her eyes. "No, and God knows where she's flitted off to *this* time." She nibbled on her manicured fingernail. "Is it about your photos?"

Matt looked at the desk and noticed that his photographs were scattered across it. "No, actually it isn't," he said, not really wanting to go into details with Tom-Tom.

"Because I might as well just tell you now that Jenna's decided she wants to go in another direction," Lucy said casually. She pushed a few of the photos to the side. "With a more established photographer."

Matt swallowed at the surprising news. "Okay."

Lucy got up and went over to the framed photographs that hung on Jenna's office wall.

She gazed over them, stopping at one of Alex in his New York Ranger uniform, holding Jenna in his lap.

"Actually, the same photographer who takes all the official shots of her sweetie pie." Lucy's gaze zoomed back to Matt. "So don't take it personally. There was just a little bias there." She let out a long sigh. "Gotta love Jenna—except for trading in football jocks for hockey hunks, she hasn't changed one iota." Then she laughed. "I'm sorry to be honest, because I think your shots are really . . . cute."

"Not a problem." Matt felt as if Lucy had thrown cold water in his face. He had thought that he and Jenna had shared something special during the photo shoot. Something . . . *Guess not.* "Thanks. Nice to see you." Matt turned to walk out.

"Listen, Matt," Lucy said hastily, throwing him a bone. "As long as you came all the way down here, why don't we go downstairs and get you your last check? If you want to sign a general release, maybe we can use your shots for a catalog, or something down the road?"

"Fine," Matt mumbled robotically.

After hearing what Lucy had just said, he'd

rip up the check anyway.

It didn't matter anymore.

● ● ●

This was it. The moment of truth. There was no music, no fancy high-tech presentation. Just the boards with Matt's photographs, Jenna's cutout text, her hand-lettered captions displayed on easels, and the blowups.

"I know it's different, I mean, from anything we've ever done, and I know you might hate it and think I'm completely crazy, but to be honest, I won't care, even if I get fired," Jenna said as she stood in front of the assembled staff. "I don't mean that disrespectfully or anything, it's just that I've realized—"

She pulled out a board that was covered with photographs of jaded, thin, weary-looking models. "Who are these women? Does anyone know? I don't recognize any of them."

She stuck one of Matt's beautiful photographs in front of it. "When I was little, I worshipped my babysitter. She was funny and confident and knew the words to every Beatles song. Where is she in these magazines? I want to see my best friend's older sister, the girls from the soccer team, my next-door neighbor—real women who are pretty and smart and happy with who they are. These are the women to look up to." Jenna took a big breath as she tried to gauge her colleagues' feelings. "So let's put some life back into our magazine. I think we all, all of us, want to feel something again that we've forgotten, or turned our backs on . . . because we didn't stop to notice how much we were leaving behind."

Jenna gasped as Richard stood up and grabbed her in a huge hug. Then he stepped back, looking into her eyes with genuine delight and appreciation. Around her, the *Poise* staff began to murmur excitedly.

Jenna realized that everyone in the room was behind her and her ideas. They all loved her redesign!

"We will present this to corporate first thing Friday morning," Richard announced. "If they don't want it, I will quit and we will start our own magazine."

"Count me in," Glenn called out.

Everyone else chimed in their agreement as well.

"Who is this Matt?" Richard asked Jenna, pulling her aside. "Is he by chance single and gay?"

Jenna blinked at her boss. "You're gay?"

To that, Richard just put his hands on his hips.

Minutes later Jenna burst through the front door of *Poise,* racing out onto the bustling New York City sidewalk. She was floating on a cloud. Not only did everyone who mattered at *Poise* think her ideas were brilliant, they thought Matt was brilliant too!

She couldn't wait to meet him tonight and share her wonderful news.

They had a redesign to celebrate!

● ● ●

Tonight wasn't any ordinary night—it was going to be the best grown-up night she'd ever had! Jenna dressed in her prettiest dress and her fanciest shoes and wore the pink satin headband Matt had given her.

On the way to Matt's apartment, Jenna passed a newsstand. Unable to stop herself, she rearranged the magazines on display, shoving all the copies of *Sparkle* to the back so that only

Poise could be seen. With a wink to the news-stand guy, she continued on her way. When it started to rain, it didn't dampen her spirits for one second.

When she got to Matt's apartment, she was giggling and dripping. *He is going to be so happy!* she thought as the door opened. But Matt wasn't behind it.

"Hi." It was Wendy. Matt's friend acted as if she couldn't remember Jenna's name. "Jenny, right?"

"Hi," Jenna said, surprised to see her. Droplets of water fell from her dress onto the floor. "I'm sorry to stop by so late. I just wanted to tell Matt some really, really great news about his photographs." She mustered a smile. "Everybody loves them!"

"That's great!" Wendy said, looking ready to close the door. "I'll tell him when he comes back. He's just picking up his tux."

"His tux?" Jenna repeated, bewildered. What did Matt need a tux for and why was he doing it tonight when they had plans together?

Wendy shook her head, *tsk-tsk*ing. "I know. Men! Everything till the last second. I mean, hello? We're getting married this Friday!"

The news hit Jenna like a ton of bricks. She knew Matt was getting married to Wendy—he'd told her that—but this weekend? *Right now?*

"Thank god for Matt's mom," Wendy chattered on. "She's doing *everything*. This is going to be the sweetest little backyard wedding since I don't know when, although personally?" She lowered her voice. "I just want to get honeymooning already!"

Jenna forced herself to smile again. "Well, congratulations."

"I'll tell Matty you stopped by."

"Thank you," Jenna mumbled as Wendy moved to close the door. "Congratulations."

And feeling the complete opposite of the way she'd felt when she arrived, Jenna turned and walked back into the rainy New York City night.

● ● ●

The next morning Jenna stood in her office, in front of her boards, and tried to muster up the enthusiasm she had felt during her presentation. Today she was to present her ideas to corporate management—she had to be at the top of her game.

Instead, she felt tired and flat. "We want to feel something—we've forgotten, turned our backs on—" she mumbled, trying to remember what exactly she had said the day before that had gotten everyone so fired up. Ever since Matt had stood her up and Wendy had closed Matt's apartment door in her face, Jenna had felt lost.

Her office door opened and Richard walked in.

"Ready?" Jenna asked, mustering a smile.

To her surprise, he closed the door. "Meeting's canceled, Jenna. It's over."

Jenna gaped at him. "What? What do you mean?"

Richard shook his head. "We're shutting down."

"Shutting down?" Jenna didn't understand.

"You know what?" Richard threw his arms up. "Screw it, who cares? I'm better than this place. *You're* better than this place. Leave the rat race to the rats. That's my new motto. I've been looking for an excuse to quit for two years, anyway."

He wasn't making sense. "But . . . but why, Richard? What happened?"

Richard looked at her as if it was obvious.

"Jenna, you must know." She shook her head. "Lucy. She's taken all your ideas with her to *Sparkle*. Everything."

"Lucy?" Jenna sputtered. "*Sparkle*? What are you talking about? I don't understand."

"You haven't heard?" Richard's voice rose to an infuriated squeak. "She's their new editor in chief. Your photos showed up in *Sparkle Online* last night; they're in outdoor ads today. They're using your whole concept."

"They can't use Matt's photos!" Jenna cried, incensed. "They can't do that!"

But Richard's gaze told her otherwise. "Jenna, they can, and they are." He pulled a piece of paper from his pocket and held it out to her.

She grabbed it. It was a photographer's release form . . . authorized by Lucy Wyman and signed by Matt Flamhaff.

Jenna raced down the hall and stormed into Lucy's office. There stood Lucy, packing her belongings into large cardboard boxes.

"How could you do this?" Jenna cried, waving the release in Lucy's face. "How could you?"

Lucy barely looked up as she carried a fancy

ashtray to a box. "Which one do you want to be today, the pot or the kettle? I think *I'll* be the pot."

"What?"

"Mmm, maybe the kettle," Lucy mused aloud. "Either way, we're both black, so spare me the huffing and the puffing."

"What are you talking about?" Jenna shouted at her.

"I'm talking about this little nugget I found in your office." Lucy waved a small envelope under Jenna's nose.

"You went through my things?" Jenna yanked the envelope from Lucy's grasp.

"Oh, how immoral of me," Lucy mocked. "How dastardly. The outrage!" She sneered. "Please."

Jenna quickly pulled out the note attached to the magazine cover. "What is this?" she said, scanning it. "I don't even know what this is!"

Lucy glared at her. "Okay, wipe that doe-eyed Bambi-watching-his-mother-get-killed look off your face, would you? I talked to Trish Sackett. She told me *all* about your little deal— a very sweet deal, by the way. Editor in chief if you helped them hit a million? So you gave them tips . . . nice, very nice." Lucy shook her head ruefully. "I wish I had thought of it myself."

Jenna looked at the cover and read the note—a note from Trish Sackett. Suddenly everything clicked into place. Her grown-up self had been betraying *Poise* before her thirteen-year-old self took over. And Lucy had found out about it.

"Oh, no," Jenna began slowly. "Oh, no."

"Oh, yes," Lucy corrected. "Only now I'm taking your job and you can stay here with the magazine you single-handedly flushed down the toilet." Turning her back on Jenna, she resumed her packing.

Jenna stood there, dumbfounded, for a moment. Then she held out Matt's release. "When did you see Matt?"

"When was it? Yesterday? The day before?" Lucy pretended to think. "I can't remember."

"Why would he sign this?" Jenna demanded, fighting back the urge to wrap her fingers around Lucy's throat and squeeze very, very tightly. "What did you *tell* him?"

Lucy shrugged. "I told him that you had decided to go in a different direction—which you are now . . . and I *may* have mentioned a few other little things."

Jenna's voice was low. "*What* other things? What did you say to him?"

Lucy dumped a framed diploma into a box and lifted her chin. "Give it a rest, Jenna. You were always one step behind me. You are so over." Pushing past her, Lucy walked out.

● ● ● nine

A bus displaying one of Matt's photos with Jenna's copy, "New York Class of 2004," advertising *Sparkle*, whizzed past Jenna on Sixth Avenue.

Seeing that bus confirmed the awful fact. Richard and Lucy had been telling the truth.

And Lucy had told Matt something awful, Jenna was certain of it.

Devastated at the thought of Matt hurting for even one moment, Jenna stood frozen on the sidewalk, a million emotions running through her mind.

Suddenly Richard and Lucy and *Poise* and *Sparkle* didn't seem very important anymore. All that mattered, Jenna realized, her heart pounding in her chest, was Matt.

The passion Jenna had felt inside these past weeks gave a little sputter and spark of hope.

Love was a battlefield. And it was time for Jenna to suit up and start fighting.

● ● ●

Jenna sprinted to the curb and expertly hailed a cab. *I've got to get there in time,* she thought as she flung herself into the taxi's stuffy backseat. Music played on the radio. *I've got to—*

"Jenna? Jenna Rink?"

Jenna looked up from her thoughts, startled. The cabdriver—a heavyset bald thirty-something guy—was staring at her in the rearview mirror.

"Yes?" she said cautiously. *How does he know my name?*

The cabdriver grinned as if he was stating the obvious. "Chris Grandy!"

Jenna's eyes shot to the driver's ID badge and photo, which hung from the plexiglass partition. Her jaw dropped. There, next to a plastic-encased photograph of a smiling, bald fat man was a yellow cab identification number and the driver's name. It *was* Chris Grandy. *The* Chris Grandy!

"Holy freakin' cow!" Chris said, shaking his head with amazement. "This is so gnarly! What have you been doing? You married? If you're single, I'm going to want a phone number."

Jenna smiled weakly as the cab sailed up the Henry Hudson Parkway. She remembered her parents talking about people going downhill since high school, but this really took the cake.

It was just her luck that there was a ton of traffic today. After the cab crossed over the George Washington Bridge into New Jersey, they got stuck behind a row of cars waiting for a train to pass.

Chris continued to talk, while Jenna pressed her face against the window, willing the traffic to disappear.

Suddenly Rick Springfield's "Jesse's Girl" came on the radio. Chris let out a whoop and turned up the radio. "Holy cripe!" he said. "Isn't this the tune we first tangled tongues to?

What's this dude's name . . . Rick Springsteen?"

All Jenna could see was an endless line of traffic at a standstill. No one was moving an inch. "Chris, what's going on?" she said, frustrated.

"Well, it looks like we got us a traffic marmalade . . . better known as a traffic jam." He chuckled. "That's my own little joke."

Without laughing, Jenna pulled a wad of cash from her bag and tossed it through the partition, hitting Chris in the side of the head. She couldn't take his tiresome chitchat or the traffic any longer. Going on foot had to be quicker, and much less painful.

"Hey, wait!" Chris yelled as Jenna jumped out of the cab and ran past the train crossing. "Don't you want my number?"

Jenna didn't look back. Even if Chris Grandy had grown up to be hot, she wouldn't have wanted his stupid number.

She already had the number of the only person she'd ever wanted.

● ● ●

Jenna ran breathlessly down her hometown's main street, past the ice cream shop, the old barbershop, and the other tiny mom-and-pop businesses, barely giving them a glance.

At last! she thought as she raced up to Matt Flamhaff's house. Just as she'd feared, the wedding party was assembled in the Flamhaffs' backyard.

Where is he? Where is he! Where—

There, up in his old bedroom, she spotted Matt through the window, struggling to put on his tuxedo pants.

Without a moment's hesitation, Jenna darted through the front door. There were her parents, talking to Matt's parents. Making sure no one saw her, she stealthily crept upstairs.

"This dress is to die for!" Jenna peeked into Mr. and Mrs. Flamhaff's bedroom and saw two bridesmaids fussing over Wendy, who was dressed in a flowing white wedding gown and lacy shoes. Jenna tiptoed past and down the hallway to Matt's room.

Thank God he had his pants on. She watched as he pulled his undershirt over his head. *Pop!* His head came into view and he froze at the sight of her.

She gave him a little wave. "Hi."

Matt looked dumbfounded. "Hey."

Jenna smiled. "Backyard looks nice."

Matt smiled back. "Yeah, you know my mom. Give her a project, and . . ." He trailed off.

Jenna swallowed, hoping she could get the words out. "I don't know what Lucy said to you, but I want you to know that whoever that was she told you about . . . wasn't me."

"It doesn't matter what Lucy said, Jenna," Matt said. "I stopped trusting her after she stole my Pop Rocks in third grade."

"I'm glad one of us was smart back then," Jenna said. She hesitated, then rushed forward, gazing directly into his brown eyes. "Matt, I am not the awful person I know I was. I don't even *know* that person. And I'd like to believe . . . I *have* to believe, that if you knew that, if in your heart you really, really knew that, you wouldn't be getting ready to marry someone right now, unless that someone was me."

"Jenna," Matt began slowly. "I won't lie to you. I've felt things the past few weeks I didn't know I could feel anymore."

A shiver raced down Jenna's spine. She listened.

"But I've realized these past few *days* that you can't just turn back time," he went on.

"But why?" she cried, crushed to the core. "Why not?"

"We move on," Matt said gently. "I've moved on, you've moved on . . . down different paths for so long . . . and we've made choices. I chose Wendy. We care about each other." Matt stopped to look out his window. "Look, we don't always get the Dream House . . . but we can get awfully close."

A tear ran down Jenna's cheek. It *was* too late. Matt was going to marry Wendy. Jenna had ruined everything.

"Please don't cry," Matt said. He opened his closet. Reaching up to the top shelf, he lifted down a large plastic-wrapped object. He pulled off the plastic, and there it was. Jenna's Dream House.

"Oh, Matty," Jenna whispered, overcome with emotion. "Can I have it? Please?"

Matt laughed. "As long as you promise not to chuck it at me again." Carefully, he handed the Dream House to her.

Now Jenna could feel a stream of tears sliding down her cheeks. There was no point trying to stop them. "Okay, I won't have you be late," she said, veering for the bedroom door. "Go, go, go! I'm crying because I'm *happy* for you. I want you to be so happy . . . so, so happy." Then she turned to face him. "I love you, Matt." She smiled through her tears. "You're my best friend."

Matt looked down at his shoes. "I've always loved you."

And, clutching the Dream House, Jenna fled.

● ● ●

Jenna didn't know what to think or feel as she walked the short distance between the Flamhaffs' backyard and her own. The sounds of soft flute music told her that the wedding was about to begin. Somehow, she'd thought that when Matt saw her, he would realize that he was supposed to be with her. *No matter how much I wish, nothing is going to change. There's no taking back the past seventeen years,* she realized, her heart broken. *No taking back the awful person I was.*

Numb, she sat down on her front steps and placed the Dream House on her knees. For the first time, she touched it and looked into each of its small, lovingly created rooms. *What have I done?* she thought.

Incredibly, after all these years, there were still tiny piles of Matt's wishing dust in the house. Jenna dipped her finger into a small snowdrift of glittering dust and examined it. *Maybe it really does have magical powers,* she thought, closing her eyes. *Maybe there is a way to go back and undo what I've done. Please let me have a chance to make things right again.*

Slowly, her heart pounding, Jenna opened her eyes.

Nothing had changed. She was still thirty. *And my heart is still broken.*

With a sigh, Jenna stood, the Dream House in her hands. How she was going to open the front door without dropping the Dream House was a mystery.

A sudden wind kicked up, blowing twigs and leaves across the Rinks' lawn. As a small swirl of leaves blew toward her feet, a gust blew them up toward her face—and sent a cloud of wishing dust swirling toward her.

"Oh!" Jenna gasped as some of the dust blew into her eyes, blinding her.

And when wishing dust mixes with the tears of a thirty-year-old woman making a wish . . . anything can happen.

Especially the wish.

● ● ●

When Jenna opened her eyes again, she wasn't standing outside. She was inside. Somewhere warm and dark. Very dark.

Could it be?

Jenna reached up and removed a blindfold. She ran her hands over her body. No boobs! Short legs in stirrup pants! She felt her hair. Hair spray and mousse! *It worked! I'm back! I'm in the closet—it's my thirteenth birthday!*

Just as it had happened before, the closet door slowly opened. But this time, Jenna wasn't sitting on the floor. She was on her feet, grinning as a nervous, anxious Matt opened the door. There he was in all his glory, with his buckteeth, braces, and thirteen-year-old baby fat!

"Matt!" she shrieked, throwing her arms around him and knocking him to the floor. She pressed her lips to his, giving him the biggest, most passionate kiss in the universe.

"Wow!" Matt said breathlessly as she pulled away. He stared at her, amazed. "You really know what you're doing!"

Just then, Lucy, aka Tom-Tom, came down the basement steps, carrying a cup of punch.

Gone were her thirty-year-old body, silky hair, and nose job. She was just a regular thirteen-year-old girl again.

"Oops," Tom-Tom said coolly. "Looks like I'm interrupting. Soooo sorry. I forgot my scarf." She reached up and plucked her scarf from around Jenna's neck.

Jenna leapt up and snatched the report proposal she had written from Tom-Tom's other hand. She ripped it promptly in two and smiled. "You know what? You can be the pot and kettle all by yourself from now on, bee-otch."

Tom-Tom's blond eyebrows drew together. "*What* did you call me?"

Jenna smacked the bottom of Tom-Tom's punch cup so that punch spilled down her dress. "Come on, Matt," Jenna said, grabbing his hand. "Let's go have some *real* fun."

We're thirteen again! Jenna thought giddily as they ran upstairs together. *It's not too late! I can make different choices—the right choices. I have the chance to make everything absolutely perfect!*

How cool was knowing that you had a

second chance . . . the power to make all the right choices in your life? And that one day you were going to grow up and be pretty and confident and nice?

Almost as cool as knowing you were going to end up marrying the sweetest guy on the planet . . . and live in your very own, very real Dream House—together.

● ● ● about the author

Christa Roberts is a pseudonym for a writer of several novels for teens. Just like thirteen-year-old Jenna Rink, she lives in New Jersey.